BUTCH

BUTCH

a novel by Jay Rayn

Boston ♦ Lace Publications

an imprint of Alyson Publications, Inc.

Typeset and printed in the United States of America.
Printed on recycled, acid-free paper.

This is a trade paperback from Lace Publications,
an imprint of Alyson Publications, Inc.,
40 Plympton Street, Boston, Mass. 02118.
Distributed in England by GMP Publishers,
P.O. Box 247, London N17 9QR, England.

Originally published by Free Women Press, May 1992.

First Alyson edition: September 1993

5 4 3 2 1

ISBN 1-55583-316-0

Library of Congress Cataloging-in-Publication Data
Rayn, Jay, 1950–
    Butch : a novel / by Jay Rayn.
      p.   cm.
    ISBN 1-55583-316-0 : $7.95
      1. Lesbians—United States—Fiction.   I. Title.
    PS3568.A935B8 1993
    813'.54—dc20   93-29580
                                                  CIP

CONTENTS

To all the butches who've dared to be,
And to the femmes who love them.

With special gratitude to
Carol Seajay of the *Feminist Bookstore News*
for helping to keep *Butch* alive.

MIKE

Valentine's Day wasn't much fun the year Mike Landetti left Silver Creek. All the girls in her class got special cards and the teacher loved her rose. But Mike was moving that day and had to leave class before beautiful Cheryl opened her poem. It wasn't an expensive card and the printing was a little messy, but even at only five years old, Michaelene Marie wanted to see Cheryl's face when she read her scrawled symbols of love.

Mike was the name she preferred, and when she arrived in Fredonia, a small college town on the shores of Lake Erie, she made sure everyone called her that. Fredonia was an Indian word meaning "free women," and that kind of freedom was important to Mike.

The new house was big, with enough yard for baseball, plenty of trees to climb, lots of hiding places, and the perfect hill for sledding. Next door was a family with three sisters, and Mike wasted no time meeting the one closest to her age. Nineteen fifty-five was a friendly year, and it wasn't long before Mike and neighbor Eileen ended their flirtation and became fast friends. It also wasn't long before the disagreements started.

"I'll only play house if I can be the father," Mike said. "And I'm not playing with silly dolls and I don't want that makeup stuff on me!"

Eileen complained to her mother. Soon, it seemed every time Mike asked if Eileen could play, Eileen's mother had a headache and needed her daughter at home.

School was a little better. Kindergarten was held in a huge room and forty-five kids watched Mike's entrance.

"After lunch, we all rest on our special rugs," the teacher said. "Find a space and listen to the music."

Mike's heart was filled with anticipation. "Can I put my rug anywhere I want to?"

"Anywhere. As long as you don't bother the others."

Mike made a beeline for the space nearest Gail. She had dark brown hair and beautiful eyes. Mike knew resting next to her would be wonderful. Placing her rug as close to Gail as possible, Mike lay her head on her hand so she could watch Gail sleep.

By the first day of spring, Mike had managed to inch her way next to Gail. Gail seemed to enjoy the occasional hugs and spoon position they shared while listening to the Lettermen.

Recess was show-off time. The playground had swings, teeter-totters, slides, and a great set of monkey bars for somersaults and flips. Mike practiced every day, always climbing faster than any of the boys.

She made sure Gail was watching whenever she did a spin or a flip, but no matter how hard she tried, Gail seemed to enjoy the company of other girls more than Mike's act. By the time school closed for the summer, Gail had moved her rug closer to Sarah. Mike rested alone.

Summer gave Mike hours of Hero comic books, lots of baseball, and two boys to play with. Steve lived across the street. Hank was just up the hill. Together, they watched "Superman" and "I Love Lucy," talked about joining the Mickey Mouse Club, and practiced baseball to see who was most like Mickey Mantle. And, of course, they fought. Not wordy, whiny girl-fights, but real, bruising, sock-'em fights that usually found Mike on top, winning.

"Say uncle or I'll rearrange your face," Mike said to a flattened Steve. She had him pinned and he knew she meant it.

"Say uncle or else," she repeated.

"Okay. Okay. Uncle."

Mike let him up and helped brush him off.

"One of these days you're gonna lose."

"Can't lose," Mike said. "I'm Superman!"

"If you're Superman, I'm Howdy Doody!"

As Steve walked away, Mike made the whooshing sound that always accompanied Superman's flights and then smacked her feet on the ground as if landing and grabbed Steve's shirt.

"Didn't see me fly, did ya? You missed it again, didn't ya?"

Steve stayed silent but winced when Mike sang the "Howdy Doody" theme song.

They shared clothespins and baseball cards to make their bikes sound like motorcycles, and Hank joined them in football, soccer, tree climbing, and racing. They played the hard games of summer that most boys play. Soon, they called themselves the Three Musketeers of Maple Avenue.

Then came "Zorro." And Lois who lived down the street on the corner.

"Let's tie her to a tree and take off her clothes." Hank was excited. Mike didn't mind the Zorro game, but it seemed silly to make Lois naked.

"Why do you want to take off her clothes?"

"Because she's a girl, dummy," Steve answered.

"Oh."

Lois joined right in, not seeming to mind the pretend Z's carved on her budding bare chest. She let the trio take off her clothes almost every day. Hank and Steve were happy. And Mike was the best with the sword.

When Hank started kissing Lois while she was tied up, Mike didn't want to feel left out. Steve didn't like the kissing part, but Mike egged him on.

11

"That was a little too hard," Lois said after Steve's kiss.

"Ha, ha! My turn!" Mike made sure her kiss was softer than Steve's. When she stepped back for Lois's approval, Lois seemed stunned.

"What'sa matter? Did she bite ya?"

Lois shook her head and stared at Mike.

"I don't want to play anymore. Someone untie me, I want to go home."

"What'd ya do, Mike?"

Hank untied Lois and they all watched her run home, a bundle of clothes dragging behind her.

"Just kissed her," Mike said.

"She probably won't wanna play Zorro anymore," Steve said.

"Yeah. Thanks a lot, Mike. Don't ya know how to kiss?"

Hank seemed really angry. Mike didn't know what to say. It wasn't even her best kiss. Hank and Steve walked away, pretending to talk only to each other but making sure Mike could overhear them.

"Probably gave her the tongue," said Hank.

"Bet she did," Steve agreed.

Mike didn't know what they meant. How could you give someone your tongue?

She hopped on her three-speed and raced by them. When Hank and Steve caught up with her at the corner, they seemed to have forgotten their anger. They all decided to gather bottles. If they took them to Sullivan's store, they could trade the deposits for cooling Popsicles.

Every summer was the same. By fourth grade, they had enough Popsicle sticks to build a fort. As they sat on Sullivan's steps talking about the Beaver and how pretty Annette was getting, Mike watched a tall blonde girl walk by. She seemed to appear at the store every time they were there.

"Her name is Sharon and she knows you're watching." Steve passed his hand in front of Mike's face to break her trance.

She watched and wondered and dreamed. This was her home. She never wanted to move again.

THE
ENGLISH
GIRL

The five-and-ten was the best place to buy jewelry, especially if you didn't have much money and wanted something shiny and rich-looking. It took her last dollar, but Mike finally found the perfect necklace for a new classmate named Mary. She raced back to Steve's house to show him her treasure.

"Why you buyin' presents for that English girl, Mike?"

Smiling, Mike dangled the rhinestones in the autumn sun.

"Don't ya know how to make girls like you? You buy them presents! Things they can show off. Didn't you see that new movie? *Gone with the Wind?*"

Steve shook his head.

"Well, we saw it at the drive-in. I fell asleep for a lot of it, but this one guy, Red Butler or something like that, really knew how to get girls to like him." She fondled the necklace.

"Betcha she'll be my girlfriend now," she said, sticking her chest out with pride.

Steve grabbed a basketball and dribbled off toward his hoop. "Let's play pig," he said.

Putting the necklace in her bike's saddlebag, Mike readied herself for the competition.

"My mom says there's something wrong with you. Chasing after girls all the time and trying to be a tomboy." He missed a lay-up.

"If I make it you get a *P*," Mike said. She took her time and did a perfect lay-up. She loved winning.

"Who says I'm trying to be a tomboy? And what's wrong with liking girls? Don't you like girls?"

She successfully made a long shot. It was Steve's turn to follow.

"I like girls all right. But I'm supposed to like 'em. You're supposed to like boys."

He sunk a long shot and then dribbled in for a side basket.

"I like boys. I like you, don't I?"

Steve missed. Mike tried it next.

"Don't I?" she asked again.

"I suppose. But my mom still says there's something wrong with you."

"*P-I*. One more and I win."

She paced off twelve steps and turned her back to the basket so she could shoot backwards.

"Maybe your mom just doesn't like girls, so she thinks I shouldn't either."

Swish! The ball went through the net without touching the hoop.

"I guess you're right," Steve said. He counted off twelve steps and turned his back to the hoop. "Dad says he likes ya. He says you're kinda cute."

"*G*. You lose."

"So, what else is new?"

"That's okay, buddy," Mike said. "You're getting better."

After tossing him the basketball, she retrieved her bike from the lawn. Putting her left foot on the lower pedal, she mounted her bike as if it were a horse, then she stood up on the pedals and made the wheels spin with her power. She raced down the driveway and slammed on the brakes so her rear wheel skidded in the gravel.

After a moment, she tiptoe-walked her bike back toward Steve.

"Do you think there's something wrong with me?"

Steve thought for a minute, made a face like Curly from the Three Stooges, and shrugged. "Nothing I can see," he said.

Mike smiled and left him in her dust.

❑ ❑

"It's a present. Just a little thing." Taking Mary's hand, Mike led her behind the gym bleachers. "Go ahead. Open it."

Mary opened the crudely wrapped box and gasped at the necklace.

"Oh. It's really pretty. But ... why are you giving it to me?"

"Because I like you."

Mike blushed a little, but quickly regained her tough exterior. She kissed Mary lightly on the cheek and, holding hands again, they emerged from the bleachers.

"Hey, boys. Look at this. The little tomboy has a girlfriend."

Leigh was the leader of the tough boys. Though Mike had beaten him up more than once, he never stopped bothering her.

"You like bein' her girlfriend?" Leigh grinned and tried to block Mary's path. Mary looked at Mike, at the boys around Leigh, and then squeezed Mike's hand.

"I like it fine. A lot more than I like you."

Leigh moved back so they could walk by. "Gee, boys," he said. "I guess we got two fags in this school."

He laughed and the others followed his lead. Mike spun around and grabbed him by the shirt.

"After school, buddy," she said.

"I'll be there."

Leigh's friends scattered to tell everyone about the fight.

15

Gym class was after lunch. Mike loved the teacher and usually loved the class, but this week was dancing lessons. She hated it. All the girls were supposed to learn how to follow the boys in a box step. Mike just couldn't do it. Every boy who tried to dance with her got pushed into following her lead. Mr. Conway, the boys' teacher, finally took Mike by the hand.

"Come with me, Michaelene. We're going to learn how to do this once and for all."

He seemed angry, but Mike wasn't worried. Mr. Conway knew she was a good athlete. He always spent extra time training her for "someday in the Olympics."

He positioned her hands, making her stiffen them while he held her.

"You do the girl's part. Follow me. When I tap your hip, that's the leg you move. Okay. Ready?"

He tapped her left hip and moved his right leg. She moved with him to avoid getting stepped on.

"That's it. Now the other. And the other. And a little faster."

They managed four or five steps before Mike started leading again. Mr. Conway didn't realize he was following her until she smiled at him in triumph. He threw his hands in the air.

"Oh, forget it." He put Mary's hand in Mike's. "Here, dance with her. She knows how to follow."

Mike couldn't believe her luck! Mary was the only one she wanted to dance with. Mr. Conway had practically pushed them into each other's arms.

When the Connie Francis record started, Mike led Mary around the gym floor. As they stepped and swayed to "Who's Sorry Now," Mike suddenly realized that everyone had stopped to watch them. Dancing was easy, and she was good at it, but the staring and whispering mixed with Connie's words made her feel different from everyone else. She listened to their snickers while she danced. Suddenly, she stopped and tore the necklace from Mary's neck.

"I'm sorry," she said. "I shouldn't have given you this."

In the chilling silence that followed, Mike's glare told Mary their brief affair was over. Mr. Conway quickly interrupted.

"Tell you what, kids. There's too much energy around here. Let's split up into even sides and have a game of war."

He quickly dug out some volleyballs. Mike and Mary were chosen for opposite teams. The object of the game was to hit your opponents with balls without them catching them (in which case you'd be out), and to either dodge or catch balls thrown at you.

Soon, Mike was the only one left on her side. Five of Leigh's gang threw balls at her, but she dodged every one.

"Catch 'em, Mike," Mr. Conway coached from the sidelines.

"Can't catch five at once," Mike shouted.

She dodged and jumped and laughed at the other team's frustration. Class ended twenty minutes later, and though exhausted, Mike was proud that she had outlasted her attackers. Making sure the necklace was secure in her pocket, she followed her classmates out of the gym. In two hours she'd face Leigh on the school lawn. She knew he'd try pulling up her skirt to embarrass her, but she felt strong and ready. No one had ever beaten her, and today was no different from any other day.

❏ ❏

The fight didn't last long. Leigh swung, snickered, tripped, and pushed. He tried pulling up Mike's skirt, but she had shorts on underneath and a power to survive that most didn't understand. She pinned his arms to the ground and tugged on his earlobes.

"Give or die."

The audience of all ages joined the chant. "Give or die! Give or die!"

"I give."

Mike jerked on his earlobes one last time before letting him roll away in shame. She pulled her white blouse out of her waistband and took off her skirt. Pants or shorts were always more comfortable. One boy brought her bike over and another her books. As Mike mounted her bike, she glanced at Mary. She was holding hands with an older boy. She seemed happy.

COUSIN
MARYJO

Mike borrowed her father's Vitalis hair tonic and combed her hair into a Fabian-like curl. Though she could mimic Avalon's voice, she thought she looked more like Fabian, especially because she was Italian. She wanted to look especially good for Christmas dinner at Landetti's restaurant. The restaurant was closed for the holidays, allowing the entire Landetti family to take over the dining room: five uncles, one aunt, her parents and grandparents, and, of course, the cousins. Mike mostly liked the bar and the jukebox, and her special cousin, MaryJo.

"Hey, Venus. Oh, Venus?" Mike loved singing to her cousin MaryJo. MaryJo was a few years older and lived a half hour's drive from Fredonia. Christmas vacation meant sleeping over at each other's house for a few days at a time, staying up later than usual, and doing things you couldn't always do at home. Mike couldn't wait to get to MaryJo's that night.

"Mom says we can have my room all to ourselves," MaryJo said. "And stay up as late as we want. What do you wanna do?"

"I don't know, Cuz. You're the oldest. You tell me what you want and I'll do it."

"I know! We'll play boyfriend and girlfriend! You pretend you're my boyfriend and we're on a date."

"Okay." Mike wasn't sure what boys and girls did on dates, but she knew MaryJo would help her learn.

"Well, ask me to dance."

"Okay. You wanna dance?"

"Not like that, silly. I'll stand over here and pretend I'm not looking at you. You play some special song on the jukebox and then ask me nicely if I want to dance."

Mike put one of her father's quarters in the box and selected a tune. She slicked back her hair, fixed the curl on her forehead, wiped her hands on the skirt her mother had made her wear, and sauntered over to her cousin.

"May I have this dance?" she asked.

"Not yet," MaryJo whispered. "The record hasn't started yet."

Volare. Oh-oh.

"Oh, what am I going to do with you? Mike, when you're asking a girl to dance you don't pick a song like 'Volare'! You pick something slow. And sexy."

"What's 'sexy' mean?"

"You know. Something that makes her dance close to you. Here. I'll pick the next one."

When the Paul Anka record started, Mike understood the difference immediately. She walked over to her cousin, took her hand without a word, and led her to the dance floor. At first, MaryJo kept her distance as Mike danced her slowly around the empty bar. Soon, she moved closer and, with a little physical coaxing from Mike, rested her head on Mike's shoulder.

Put your head on my shoulder.
Whisper in my ear, baby.
Words I long to hear, baby.
Tell me that you love me, too.

20

They played their game right up to bedtime.

"So, how'd you like the date?" Mike asked.

"It's not over yet. You have to try to kiss me good night."

"But we're already in bed."

"That's okay. My friends at school say some boys stay overnight. Just pretend you are and kiss me good night."

Mike leaned over her cousin's smiling face and kissed her gently on the lips. MaryJo pulled her down and kissed her again. And again. And again.

"I love you," MaryJo said.

"Of course you love me. You're my cousin."

"But I mean I really love you. I wish you were really my boyfriend."

MaryJo snuggled into Mike's arms, crying a little. Mike held her close and petted her head.

"I can't be a boy for you, but I can love you like one if you want me to. I don't know why girls think they have to have boyfriends, anyway."

MaryJo stopped crying, but snuggled closer and wrapped her arm around Mike's waist. "Because you can't marry another girl," she said.

"Why not? I could marry you."

"You can't. People won't let you do that. Anyway, I want to have kids someday and I know you can't do that. And, by the way, you can't tell anyone about our game. My mother would have fits if she knew we were kissing."

"Do you wanna do it some more?" Mike rolled over on one elbow and ran her fingers down her cousin's cheek. "We can kiss all night if you want to."

MaryJo smiled and Mike kissed her deeply. They both wished Christmas would come more than once a year.

NEWTON
STREET

As the weather turned warmer, Mike got home from school later and later. Spring always made her a little crazy. Sharon was making it even worse. Instead of riding her bike home the usual way, she followed Sharon to her house and stayed as long as possible.

"You know, we used to watch you walking by Sullivan's."

"I know."

Sharon was almost a foot taller than Mike, with long blonde hair and green eyes. Her sister, Peggy, was more Mike's size, but she was older than Mike and not as friendly. Mike thought up every excuse imaginable so that she could spend more and more time with Sharon. She rode along the curb while Sharon walked on the sidewalk, always careful to keep her distance. In some ways, she was afraid of this girl. She felt something powerful and mysterious whenever she was close to her. It was like the feelings she had for MaryJo, but much stronger. She was afraid she wouldn't be able to control herself if they ever touched.

"Wanna listen to some records?" Sharon invited Mike into her den and closed the door.

"Uh, no. No. If you want to you can but, I don't really feel like..."

"Why don't you sit here?"

Sharon pushed Mike into an overstuffed chair and smiled.

"I never thought you would be so shy," Sharon said. "You always act so tough and in control."

"I'm tough. I'm also a little shy."

"My friend Kathy hates you, you know? She says you act too much like a boy and I should stay away from you."

"Why is she your friend?"

"Because my mother wants her to be. Do you like Connie Francis?"

Mike squirmed in the chair. "She's okay. I like the Everly Brothers and Anka more, though."

"Oh. I don't know them very well. My sister likes them, if you wanna pick one out."

Mike got up, relieved that she didn't have to feel trapped in the chair anymore. She didn't bother to look at the song titles, she just grabbed a Paul Anka label and put it on the record player. Sharon sat waiting on the arm of the chair. Mike was scared to death. She put her hands in her pockets and pretended to look at pictures on the tiny room's walls. Suddenly, Sharon's hand grabbed her arm and pulled her back to the chair.

"Why don't you sit down so we can listen together?"

Mike sat. Feeling the heat from Sharon's body, she pushed herself way down into the cushions. When the record started, Mike's throat closed tight.

Put your head on my shoulder...

They listened in silence. Mike didn't dare look at Sharon. She prayed for a scratch in the record or a knock on the door. The tension in her legs made one knee start bouncing and she slapped her hand on it to make it stop.

23

Then she was there. Right in her lap. Mike felt the weight of Sharon's tall slimness and closed her eyes tightly when Sharon's long arms wrapped around her neck.

"Sing it to me," Sharon said.

Mike couldn't find her breath. She opened her eyes to Sharon's smiling face and then crunched them closed again. She tried to turn away, but Sharon's arms encircled her. Finally, the record ended and Mike could breathe again. But Sharon didn't move.

"Didn't know which one I put on," Mike said nervously. "You wanna go for a walk or something?"

Still smiling, Sharon shook her head. Then the same song started again. Mike had forgotten to swing over the replay arm. All she could hope for now was a knock on the door. But deep inside, she wanted what Sharon wanted. And so instead of fleeing, she put her arm around Sharon's back. Immediately, Sharon settled in and Mike knew it was too late to stop. Finding her courage, Mike looked at Sharon lovingly. Slowly, slowly, they neared each other. Mike could feel the gentle warmth of Sharon's lips. She pulled Sharon closer. And closer. Until neither of their bodies could breathe separately.

The kissing lasted through eleven replays. Only when Sharon thought she heard her mother walking by the den did she rise to stop the repetition. Mike felt exhausted. She tried to tell Sharon she'd see her tomorrow, but all she could manage was a few murmurs and "hmmms."

After leaving the house, she lingered in the side yard thinking and feeling everything and nothing. It was almost dark and had started raining when she saw the upstairs light go on. She watched Sharon's shadow undress and then dress again. Though Mike usually slept in her underwear, she supposed Sharon probably wore some kind of nightgown. She watched and listened and wondered how this girl who was almost a woman had somehow managed to bond herself to Mike's heart.

Without warning, Sharon appeared at the window, shading her eyes to see out into the darkness. She threw a kiss and pulled the shade. Mike knew she was in love.

Mike's parents weren't as happy about her day. Her mother yelled until Mike's ears hurt and her father's rage scared her more than ever before. She hadn't said anything about Sharon, but somehow they knew.

"You think more of your damn girlfriends and cronies than you do about this family! How dare you come home at all hours with that stupid curl and those sloppy jeans." Mrs. Landetti grabbed Mike's t-shirt. "And look at this. A boy's shirt on my daughter. You're old enough to start wearing bras, for God's sake!"

That did it. "No way!" Mike screamed. "I'll never wear one of those things!"

Mrs. Landetti surveyed her daughter with a smirk.

"What are you going to do when you start bleeding? Girls bleed, you know. And you're a girl. What are you gonna do then? Run around with Steve and Hank?"

Mike had no idea what she was talking about. Why in the world was she going to bleed? And from where?

"You'll see," her mother continued. "No more gym class. No more climbing trees and staying out with your cronies. The time will come."

Mike spent the rest of the night trying to figure out this bleeding thing. She had never seen her mother bleed. Mary-Jo hadn't said anything about it. She wanted to ask her cousin to explain it, but remembered that MaryJo had a boyfriend now and was usually too busy talking to her friends on the phone. She decided to ask Steve the next day.

"My mother says I'm gonna bleed because I'm a girl. Does your mother bleed?"

"I don't know," Steve said. "I guess so. I've seen her come back from the store with some strange things that my father won't buy. Maybe they're special bandages or something."

"But where does she bleed from?"

"Beats me. Maybe from her heart. I heard her call my aunt a bleeding heart once."

Hank came into the yard carrying a bat and baseball.

"They're practicin' in the athletic field. You two comin'?"

"Can't. Mike's bleeding."

Mike punched Steve hard in the arm. "I am not! And besides, bleeding wouldn't stop me from playing baseball." She grabbed the bat from Hank and ran toward the field.

"Heard you got a new girlfriend," Hank yelled.

Mike stopped and swung the bat up on her shoulder. "Heard from who?"

"From Kathy. Sharon's friend. Boy, is she jealous! She says she's going to tell Sharon's mother."

"Tell her what?" Steve asked. "What'd you do, Mike? What did she do?"

"We didn't do anything." Mike kept her eyes to the ground, remembering the day before.

"That's not the way Kathy tells it. She says Sharon's in love with you and wants to go steady."

Mike felt the heat fill her face. She hadn't expected Sharon to tell anyone. Their time had been too special, too real.

"I don't care what Kathy says. You believe everything you hear?"

Hank faced her defiantly. "I believe it about you," he said. "The guys at school will believe it."

"Keep your mouth shut." Gripping the bat in anger, Mike stood ready for Hank's attack. "It's none of your business so just shut up!"

"Wanna make me?"

Mike threw the bat to the ground and grabbed the front of Hank's shirt with both hands. As they spun each other around, Mike was surprised at how much stronger Hank was getting. She tripped him, knocking him to the ground.

"Grab her, Steve. Don't just stand there!"

Mike and Hank circled each other, their hands ready.

"Come on, Steve. Grab 'er! We can feel her up!"

When Mike looked at Steve, Hank caught her off balance. He tossed her to the ground and jumped on top of her, pinning her arms with his knobby knees. Mike fought to throw him off and almost had him, but Steve straddled her legs and held her.

26

"Go ahead," Steve said. "Feel her up and get it over with."

Hank grabbed Mike's small breasts through her shirt and squeezed them hard.

"See," he said. "This is what boys do to girls. Makes me horny. Does it make you horny?"

Mike pushed against them with all her rage, finally knocking them to the side. She lunged at Hank and trapped him in a choke hold.

"Stop it, Mike, you're killing him. Mike, let go."

Steve tried to pull her off, but Mike's anger was in control.

"Mike, come on. He can't breathe."

She could feel Hank gasping beneath her arm, but she didn't care. She hated him now. Hated him and her body and all the things that made loving Sharon wrong.

"I'll tell my mother, Mike. Let him go. Let him go!"

Not wanting any more trouble, Mike released her hold. Hank slumped to the ground. She kicked the bat toward him and then spat at his feet.

"Go play with yourself, bastard."

❏ ❏

Mike rode her bike for hours, up and down the hills, through the college streets, by the creek, the cemetery, Lafayette Park, up and down, back and forth, and finally, to Sharon's house. She propped her bike against a tree and put her feet up on the handlebars. A part of her wanted to cry, but another was just plain mad.

Though she hoped Sharon would see her and come out to be with her, she wasn't sure if she wanted to see Sharon. Just as she had made up her mind to leave, Sharon opened the door.

"What are you doing out there? Wanna come in?"

Mike just stared at her handlebars. She heard the door close and felt Sharon coming closer. She wanted to pedal away as fast as she could, but she also wanted to show Sharon how much she loved her. Sharon touched the bike, and then her soft, soft voice touched Mike's heart.

"Let's go for a walk," Sharon said.

Leaving Mike's bike by the tree, they walked up Newton Street. The packing plant was quiet, with no smell of grapes or tomatoes. The Catholic church was quiet. And even though it was Saturday afternoon, there wasn't any traffic. Sharon started humming the Anka song.

"Please don't do that," Mike said.

Sharon took her arm and kept humming. They strolled past the cemetery, then turned back and walked in. The old part had headstones from the 1800s. Mike liked the peacefulness she felt. Sharon held her arm and moved her body closer. Soon, Mike let her hand hold Sharon's and they both held tight.

They settled close together on some grass near a large maple tree and stared at the markers around them.

"I wish you hadn't told anyone," Mike said.

"I couldn't help it. I had to tell someone. I think I love you."

"If you thought you loved me you wouldn't have told."

"I wouldn't tell now."

Sharon shivered a little as it got darker. Mike put a tenuous arm around her.

"I wanna marry you," Mike said.

Sharon touched Mike's face. "I want to marry you, too."

Mike pulled her closer and kissed with all the breath in her heart. Sharon slid to the ground so Mike could cover her with her body.

"I don't know what's wrong with me," Mike said. "I feel like I have to love you. Have to give to you. I feel like I ... like I want to..."

"Make love to me."

Mike gasped and kissed Sharon again. Again and again. She rubbed her leg back and forth between Sharon's legs. Up and down. Back and forth. "Will you marry me?" Mike whispered.

"I will. I love you. I will."

When the weather was bad, they stayed in the den. On warm days, they sneaked to the cemetery. Every night, Mike waited outside until Sharon threw a kiss and pulled the shade. Every day, Mike brought a present: wildflower bouquets wrapped in Popsicle wrappers, a rose every Sunday, a new record that spoke her words of love. Finally, Mike saved enough money to buy a ring.

"It's not gold, but I wanted you to have it."

Sharon took the ring and held it close to her heart.

"Does this mean we're married?"

"I guess it's as close as we can get."

"Oh, Mike, put it on me. Please put it on me."

Mike slid the ring on Sharon's finger.

"Sharon, I'll love you forever and ever. I'll never hurt you, never leave you, never not love you. Forever and ever."

Their eyes met for a moment and Mike wiped a tear from Sharon's cheek. Then Sharon grabbed her and kissed her hard, right in front of God and everybody.

"I'll be back in a minute," Sharon said, running to her house.

"Where are you going?"

"I have to tell my mother we're married!"

"Sharon, no..."

Mike tried to warn her, but Sharon was already inside. Through the window, Mike could see Sharon talking to her mother. She watched Sharon present her hand. She watched Sharon's mother slap her daughter in the face. She heard the screams. Sharon disappeared and her mother came to the downstairs window.

"You get out of here, Michaelene Landetti. And don't come back. You leave my daughter alone! I don't want to see you around here anymore! Get out! Go home! Get out!"

The window slammed. The curtains closed. Mike stared at the house, her body frozen in anguish. Slowly, her gaze traveled the deep green boards until it fixed on Sharon's window. She heard Sharon's mother yelling, calling Sharon dirty. She heard a door slam. Through clouded eyes she watched and waited. Then the house became quiet and dark. Mike couldn't take her eyes off the window. She wanted to rush inside and whisk Sharon away. She wanted to be a boy so everything would be okay. She wanted to hold Sharon in her arms, soothe her, take away the hurt. She waited and waited. Finally, there was a light. Sharon blew a kiss, hugged herself, and drew the shade. Mike cried.

They tried to meet whenever possible, but they were never alone. Sharon's mother kept a watchful eye and instructed Kathy to stay close to them. Mike still followed Sharon home, and though they could never touch, she still felt Sharon's love. She left flowers on Sharon's steps for almost two years. Then Sharon changed schools. They hardly ever saw each other after that.

Once, she found Sharon home alone and she waited outside. But when she came to the window, Mike felt her coldness.

"Wait there," Sharon said. "I have something I want you to hear."

Sharon brought the record player close to the window, started it, then moved back, her arms crossed in front of her. "Cathy's Clown" tore through Mike's heart. The Everly Brothers sang with all the sadness and grief that Mike felt.

> *Don't want your love, anymore.*
> *Don't want your kisses, that's for sure.*

When it was over, Sharon said good-bye and closed the window. "Cathy's Clown" was embedded in Mike's soul.

JUNIOR
MISS

Mike changed her hairstyle to the dry look and adapted herself to high school. She hung out with friends who were girls and boys who she thought were friends. Steve now spent his time dating. Hank played with a band that mimicked the Beatles. Mike's life had changed drastically.

After Sharon closed the window, Mike spent the night and part of the next day at the cemetery. She could just about see Sharon's house from the maple tree. She cried and shook and remembered and cried some more. She didn't think about going home, or what would happen when she got there. She only knew she had to heal, and she couldn't do that with anyone else.

She hugged the ground where they had made love. She softly sang "Dream, Dream, Dream," wishing that Sharon could hear.

She didn't remember leaving. She didn't even know she was home until she felt her mother's slap.

"That's it, young lady. You're out. I told your father and I'm telling you. Either you go or I go."

Mike's father led her back out the door. "Don't come back. You've hurt your mother enough."

Her mother gave her a paper bag. In it was a skirt, a blouse, socks, and a t-shirt.

"There's your things. Anything else is up to you."

The door slammed. At thirteen, Mike was on her own.

❑ ❑

She mostly slept in the cemetery, where it was safe, and washed her clothes at friends' houses. She picked berries, weighed grapes, scrubbed floors, worked in the library, and washed dishes to make her way.

The worst time was winter. There was no real shelter in the cemetery, and Mike didn't have enough money for warm clothes. Often, she found a porch or back room to sleep in. Every day, she went to school and stayed as late as possible.

Christmas came and went. Mike tried calling her cousin, but couldn't reach her. No one was allowed to help. People in town knew she was alone, but when they tried to intervene, Mike's mother warned them against aiding and abetting a minor. Some still insisted on helping, but Mike didn't want others involved.

Eventually, Mike found a job as a waitress and a room above a fish market on the bad side of town.

"This is neat, Mike," Gus said. "I'd like to have my own apartment."

Mike moved the old coats from the couch to make room for her friend.

"No heat, huh?"

Mike shook her head.

"My mother says you can stay over sometimes, if ya want. Maybe I could stay over here once in a while."

"No room on the couch."

Gus's given name was Carol. Her nickname came from a shortened version of her last name. Mike didn't know how they had become friends. Maybe it was because their lockers were next to each other. Maybe it was because they were both Italian. Maybe it was just because Mike needed her.

Whatever the reason, Mike felt Gus was a true friend, someone she could rely on, laugh with, cry to if necessary. Someone she wasn't in love with.

Gus belonged to a popular sorority, Tau Kappa Omega. The girls in it were tough but not crazy. They threw parties and most had boyfriends, but many played basketball at the local CYO and had gone to Catholic grammar school. Mike felt at home with them and spent a lot of time finding ways to show how much she liked them.

Nineteen sixty-four brought more change. Older friends were going to Vietnam, some were never coming back. People shouted "Peace" and "Love" at every school assembly. Mike worked hard to survive, but wasn't sure where she fit in.

Everyone loved the Beatles. Though Mike liked them too, she still sang the old songs whenever she could and longed for the freedom of being a kid. It wasn't easy.

By her junior year, work, school, the cold loneliness of her home, and the feeling of not belonging had pushed her into a deep sadness. Then she heard Sharon's sister had been killed in a car accident.

She ran to Newton Street with new strength, strength she wanted to share. She bravely knocked on the door. When Sharon answered, Mike saw death in her face.

"I heard," Mike said. "I'm sorry."

"Thank you."

They stood silently at the door. Mike wanted to reach out to Sharon, to hold her and make everything better, but she held back.

"I have to go," Sharon said. "Thanks for coming."

"But, isn't there something I can do? To help? Or make you feel better?"

"You already have, Mike. Good-bye."

❑ ❑

Mike finished her clown makeup and walked to the super-market for work. All the cashiers and stock boys had to dress up for Halloween, but no one took it as seriously as Mike. She wanted people to smile and have fun. Her Emmet Kelly costume was a hit. She worked overtime to take care of the long lines at her register. Everyone wanted the clown.

"Excuse me. Are you entered in the Junior Miss Pageant?" Mike shook her head at the beautiful woman in line.

"Well, my name is Barbara. I used to sing with a band in New York and I'm a chaperon for the pageant. Here's my number. You really should try."

Mike took Barbara's card and bagged her groceries in role-playing silence. A beauty pageant wasn't something she had ever considered. She almost laughed at the thought of parading up and down a platform while dressed in an evening down. She'd cover it for her school newspaper column, but she wasn't going to enter.

Tryouts were the following week. Mike sat three rows back in the school auditorium so she could take notes on the competition.

"I know who you are."

Barbara sat down next to her and they watched a dozen girls recite their histories.

"You could go to college on a scholarship. And you're certainly as good as or better than anyone I've seen."

"It's not for me. I just write about it."

"I'd help you. Tell you what, I'll give you a ride home and we can talk. I know where you live. West Hill. Over the fish market, right?"

Mike nodded.

"That's a forty-minute walk and a ten-minute ride."

"How do you know where I live?"

"I asked some people. Everyone seems to know where you live."

They were watching the first six girls demonstrate calisthenics when Barbara laughed. "I even know about the garbage incident."

"I didn't know it was a fish smokehouse," Mike said. "Guess the owner lost a lot of customers."

"I know. And I think it's wonderfully innocent of you."

"I do a lot of innocent things," Mike said as they got into the car.

"Tell me, tell me. I love funny stories."

"Well, one time, when I was still living at home, my father brought home the groceries and started cooking us a spaghetti dinner. He asked me to unpack the groceries and set the table. Well, inside the grocery bag was a box of napkins. A kind I'd never seen before."

"Oh, no," Barbara laughed. "I know what you're going to say."

Mike smiled. She liked this woman. She had a great grin and a warm laugh.

"Well, I thought they were special for spaghetti. You know, the flaps on each side to tie under your chin, and the blue line down the middle so you could line up the fork? I proudly set six places with those napkins. Well, old Dad turned around, jumped at the sight of those six napkins, and spilled a whole spoonful of sauce down the front of him."

Barbara laughed again. "I bet Al was embarrassed."

"You know my father?"

"Oh, sure. Your mother does my hair."

"So that's it." Mike was angry. "My mother put you up to this. You can let me out."

"Now wait a minute, Miss Hothead. Your mother had nothing to do with this."

She pulled the car to the curb and grabbed Mike's arm.

"I know talent when I see it. And I just happen to know your story. I'm not that much different from you, you know. I sometimes love a little too much and help a little too much. People are sometimes more important to me than they should be. You're in a one-horse town over a fish market and no one around to help you get out. I want to help."

"The Junior Miss Pageant won't do it."

"Maybe it will and maybe it won't. At least you could try."

"I don't look good in clothes like that. I don't have the money those girls do. I'd just look silly."

"You have friends. Friends who love you dearly. We'll find a way. How 'bout it?"

While waiting for an answer, Barbara hummed a tune Mike didn't know.

"I'll have to think about it. What song is that?"

"'There, but for the Grace of God, Go I.'"

Barbara sang and Mike fell in love with her voice. She'd do the stupid pageant. She wanted to be near this woman, to know her. The pageant seemed like a good way to do it.

❑ ❑

Mike couldn't attend most of the rehearsals, but she met with Barbara late at night and they talked until early morning. Gus loaned her a gown and Barbara said she'd do her hair.

"This whole thing makes me feel ... I don't know, kind of..."

"Queer?"

"I guess so."

"Do you know what a queer is?"

"Not really, but I know I feel like one."

Barbara laughed. "You are a funny duck. We finally get you dressed up like a real high school girl and you feel queer."

"It's just not me."

"Well, it'll be you up on that stage. Which reminds me. You still haven't told me what you're doing in the talent competition. This is dress rehearsal. We have to know."

"I'm not sure. I guess the curtain should be closed with a spotlight on. I need a set of drums, a saxophone, and a clarinet behind the curtain. Tell the pit band to follow my lead. And pray I come up with something by tomorrow night."

"Don't embarrass me, kid."

❑ ❑

Mike had to work until an hour before the pageant. She rushed to the school and tried to change as fast as she could. She hid behind the last locker so no one would see any part of her. The other girls were nervous and scared. They dropped things, tripped over clothes they'd thrown on the floor, and complained bitterly that their makeup wasn't done right. Mike helped each feel better. "You look beautiful," she said to one.

"You'll be great," she said to another.

She helped them with their makeup and told jokes to calm them down.

"There you are!" Barbara stomped into the room in more of a panic than any contestant. "Do you know what you're doing yet? Are you ready?"

"I don't know exactly," said Mike. "But I'm good at winging things. Stop worrying. I won't let you down."

Barbara put her hand on Mike's shoulder and smiled warmly. "I love who you are, my dear little innocent one. I know I'll be proud."

❑ ❑

All the contestants did well in gymnastics and evening gown. Though Mike had never worn high-heeled shoes, she managed to walk gracefully down the aisle with her big number ten pinned to her chest. She recognized most of the judges. Two had daughters in the competition. All of them were from the right side of town. Barbara stood in the wings watching every step. She pulled her face into a smile to remind Mike to do the same and clasped her hands to show she was praying. Mike had to laugh. Poor Barbara was working harder than she was.

The talent competition was next. Two girls sang, one twirled a baton, another danced, one playacted a scene from *Macbeth*. As Mike needed more stage than anyone else, it was easiest to have her go on last.

She borrowed a guitar from the music room and took her seat in front of the curtain. The spotlight came on, but she could still make out Gus and the rest of the TKO girls in the front row. She strummed and thought and then let something inside take over.

"I am an island, alone. Amidst the great waters of people. But, now and then, a small wave of friendship laps unto the shore."

The song was going beautifully, but Mike felt it was time for something else. She pretended to break a string on the guitar. The audience gasped, but Mike held back her smile.

She plucked the string again and watched her friends cover their faces. She had them. Now she could go on.

"That something like this happened, a surprise it's surely not. It all depends on what you have. And what you haven't got."

She continued her rhymed soliloquy as she walked gingerly across the stage and motioned for the attendant to raise the curtain. She heard the audience breathe again as they realized her joke. She smiled back at them with a punch in her eyes.

Approaching the drums first, she played a portion of "Wipe Out." When the audience became involved in the beat, she flipped a drumstick behind her as if it had broken. Continuing her rhyme, she moved to the saxophone. When a mellow "Strangers on the Shore" poured over the crowd, they applauded. Barbara jumped up and down in the wings. Then Mike made a horrible sound on the saxophone. This time, the crowd laughed. They knew it was planned. Her last rhyme took her to the clarinet. She began "When the Saints Go Marching In," and the pit band joined her as she danced across the stage. The lighting crew added to the finale by flickering the colored lights. The whole auditorium rose in thunderous applause. The band did a replay and everyone, especially the TKO girls, clapped and stomped their feet. When Mike finished, the crowd called her back three times. Barbara cried. Gus cried. And Mike smiled.

The votes were in. All the contestants waited in their evening gowns for the results. Mr. Sears, a history teacher and the pageant's emcee, straightened his tuxedo before retrieving the judges' envelopes.

"The first winner we have tonight is for Miss Con- geniality. This is voted on by all the girls in competition and is given to the girl who displays the most friendship and sportsmanship in the contest. And the winner is ... number ten! Michaelene Landetti!"

Mike heard Barbara scream in the wings as she walked across the stage to receive her trophy. Mr. Sears tried to kiss her, but she shook his hand and quickly returned to her place.

"The next winner," he said, "is for the talent competition. This is a five-hundred-dollar prize awarded to the girl who displayed the best talent."

Barbara crossed her fingers. Gus made the sign of the cross.

"And the winner is ... number seven! Evelyn White! For her baton-twirling routine!"

Evelyn White accepted her prize and a kiss from Mr. Sears. Many in the crowd booed the decision. Mike could see Gus wiping her eyes.

"Now, for third place. A seven-hundred-and-fifty-dollar prize. Number two! Sally Draper!"

Sally bowed and curtsied her way to center stage, then threw a kiss to the judges, especially her mother.

"Second place and runner-up in tonight's competition goes to number five! Karen Davis! One thousand dollars!"

Everyone waited breathlessly as the drums rolled for the final announcement. Barbara kept pointing at Mike, indicating that she had won. Gus and the sorority readied confetti and flowers to throw on stage.

"The prize of two thousand dollars for the first Junior Miss of Fredonia goes to the lovely and talented ... number ... eleven! Martha Seymour!"

The audience applauded respectfully and Mike watched Barbara sink to her knees. She had let her down. When she eyed the judges' table, Mrs. Seymour mouthed the words, "Good job. It was very close."

After the curtain came down, Barbara rushed on stage to give Mike the tightest embrace she'd ever had.

"My wonderful, lovely dear. You should have won. You should have! My sweet, wonderful girl!"

She squeezed Mike's cheeks and kissed her, then hugged her again.

"It's all politics. Small-town politics. You were wonderful! Perfect! Let's go! There's a big party at the Inn and you're going!"

Barbara practically dragged her through the crowd. Gus was waiting by the door, still crying.

"Wait a minute, Barbara. There's someone I have to see."

"Certainly, sweetie. But don't try to change out of that gown! This is a dress-up party!"

Mike put an arm around Gus's shoulder. "Sorry I didn't win," she said.

"You won. The judges may not know it, but you won."

Mike hugged her crying friend. "Can I stay at your house after the party tonight? I don't feel like going home alone."

"I was going to ask you to come. I just can't stop crying."

"It's the Italian in you, Gus. Makes you all emotional about stuff."

She gave Gus one more hug before leaving with Barbara for the Inn. She really didn't want to go. The pageant parents were out of her league and she felt so uncomfortable in the gown; but Barbara wanted her there and Mike would do anything to please her.

The Inn was crowded and stuffy. When Mike and Barbara made their entrance, everyone spontaneously applauded. Mike wished she had won so the applause wouldn't hurt so much. Dance music started and Barbara pulled Mike across the room.

"There's someone very special who would like to have the first dance with you."

As they moved through the throng, people patted Mike's shoulder and shook her hand. Then the crowd parted — and there was Mike's father, smiling proudly.

"Al. Your daughter."

Al took Mike's hand and gently led her to the dance floor. People watched, whispered, smiled, and cried.

"Hi, Dad," Mike said. "Sorry I didn't win."

As "Turn Around" played quietly, Al lovingly danced his daughter around the floor. Mike had no trouble following him. He was a good leader.

"Is Mom here?"

"She couldn't make it. But I'm sure she'd be proud."

They finished the dance and stood politely next to each other.

"It's my turn!" A slightly drunk Barbara took Mike's hand.

"I have to go anyway," Al said. Mike saw tears in his eyes when he kissed her forehead. "Mom will be expecting me."

Slowly pulling the sparkling number from her chest, Mike watched him leave.

"Give this to him someday," she said to Barbara. "So he'll remember."

Barbara took the number. "But aren't you going to stay?"

"I need to get back to me, Barbara. I'll call you."

Mike patted Barbara's back to stop her from crying.

"Just remember I love you, dear thing. I'm very proud."

"I love you, too. As much as I can."

BOOT
CAMP

Mike stayed at Gus's house until their relationship grew too painful. They were hugging too often in their sleep and Gus had a boyfriend who didn't like Mike very much.

Mike kept herself busy by joining every extracurricular school activity available: band, the school newspaper, yearbook, intramural sports. It was her way of blending in and it kept her away from her lonely West Hill home. In five months, she'd have her diploma. She wanted to graduate, but she didn't know what her future held. Everyone she knew was planning on college, but it was too expensive for Mike to think about. The only chance she had was a regents' scholarship, and that would take a lot of study time.

"Michaelene. I want you to come with me."

Mike looked up from the boxes she was stacking to see her uncle Charlie.

"Hi! What's going on?"

"Just come with me, honey. I told your boss you had to leave. He understands."

"Did something happen? Is everyone okay?"

"Everyone's fine. You're going to live with me in East Aurora so you won't have to go to a wayward home."

"Wayward home? What are you talking about? I have my own place. On West Hill!"

"Too many people in town complained to the authorities about you. If your parents won't take you back and there are no other relatives, you'll have to go to a wayward home until you're eighteen."

"Complained about what?" Mike threw the boxes on the floor and readied her fists. "What the hell did I do now?"

"You didn't do anything. People felt sorry for you so they tried to help. It's okay, honey. You'll be in the school where I teach music. It's better this way."

Mike slowly took off her supermarket smock and carefully folded it.

"I have to see some people first. I'll meet you."

"Be back in one hour. We have to get started."

❏ ❏

While waiting for Gus at the sub shop, she played pinball to clear her mind.

"Hey, buddy! What's up?"

Gus was in a great mood, but Mike saw her eyes change as soon as she looked at her.

"I have to leave."

"What do you mean you have to...?"

"It's a long story. I'll be in East Aurora. Here's the address. I'll be back. I promise I'll be back to graduate here."

Mike held in her own tears as she comforted her shaking friend.

"It's not a big deal. As soon as I'm eighteen I'll come back."

"You can't go away. You're my best friend. I ... I think I love you or something."

Mike managed a smile. "I think I love you or something, too. And that won't stop. Just write to me. Tell the others to write, too."

She pulled Gus close to her, hugging her warmly. "I won't stop loving you, Gus," she whispered. "I'll be back. Wait for me and I'll be back. I love you. I really do."

She held the hug a moment longer and then walked out without another glance.

❑ ❑

The school in East Aurora was run-down and old. It was too late for Mike to register for regular classes, so she took a lot of study halls and business courses. Her birthday was three months away, but it seemed an eternity.

"The mailman's starting to complain," Charlie said. "My Lord! You must get twenty letters a day!

"Guess people don't want me to feel lonely."

"You have to let go, Mike. Make a new life here. New friends. Start over again."

"Doesn't seem much need to restart something you never really had."

"Oh, now you're feeling sorry for yourself. Your mother's a sick woman! She can't help what she does. Four kids and not enough money. Working too hard all her life. You're the toughest kid she has. If anyone can make it through this, you can. Toughen up!"

"I'm tough enough. And I don't blame my mother. She's just a woman doin' the best she can. But I'm going back on my birthday. I'm quitting high school and going back. No one can stop me once I'm eighteen."

"Oh, Mike. That's foolish. You need to graduate. You'll never get anywhere if you don't have a diploma."

"I'll graduate. But with my class. The same people I've been with since kindergarten."

The letters came every day and every night Mike wrote back. Gus sometimes sent two or three at a time and Mike noticed they always had "SWAK" on the envelope.

"I guess I have to tell you something, Gus," she wrote in one letter. "It makes me cry a little when I see the 'Sealed with a Kiss' on the back of your letters. I know it's a song, and I know you probably mean it, but absence makes the

44

heart grow fonder, or so they say. Sometimes I wish I really could kiss you. I wish I was sleeping in your bed again, and hugging you, and feeling warm and loved. Does that sound awful to you?"

Gus wrote back and the letter had "SWAK" scribbled all over it. Mike took it to her room and stared at the envelope. She was afraid she had ruined their friendship. She was afraid this would be Gus's last letter to her.

Dear Mike,
First of all, nothing you could ever do or say would sound awful to me. I wish the same things you do. Really. I used to worry about it because the nuns always said those feelings weren't normal. But I know I do love you. More than I could ever love anyone. It's just that I also love Tony. We're supposed to be married someday. I don't want to hurt him. Or hurt my family. I wish it was different. I wish you were a boy so all these feelings I have for you would be natural. But you're not. So let's just stay friends. And know that I do love you. Come back soon.

Mike thought that maybe deep inside she really was a boy. Maybe that's why she always fell in love with girls. She had read an article about a man who got an operation to become a woman. Maybe she could do the same thing. But she didn't want to be a boy. A penis wasn't something she dreamed about or longed for. God, she didn't even think penises were good-looking! Women were more beautiful, inside and out. She liked her body. She also liked the boyishness of it: the muscles, the leanness. She knew she must be the only one in the world who had this problem. Everyone else, she was sure, was doing all the normal things, all the boy and girl things, they were supposed to do.

❑ ❑

The letters continued until the middle of March. On the twentieth, Mike kept her promise. She quit high school, said good-bye to her uncle, and hitchhiked back to Fredonia. It took three days to convince the principal to let her back into school. The regents' exams were in two weeks. She put off seeing Gus until the school thing was settled. As soon as it was, they met each other by the lake.

Gus stood motionless by her car. Mike wasn't sure how to act. Letters were one thing, but seeing Gus was another. She wanted to run to her and hold her, but she wasn't sure Gus would accept that. Slowly, they walked to each other. Slowly, they took each other's hands. They hugged and cried and hugged some more. Neither would let go or pull away. Mike almost kissed her on the lips, but stopped herself. Gus almost kissed her back, but turned away in time.

"I told you I'd come back. I never break a promise."

❏ ❏

When Mike got the results of her exams, she headed straight for the guidance office.

"What do the numbers mean? How'd I do?"

"It means you scored in the top five percent. It means you'll get a scholarship to college!"

"I wanna stay right here. Can we check out Fredonia State?"

"Why don't you wait outside, Mike? I can make a phone call or two and see how it looks."

While she waited, her favorite teacher came in to congratulate her.

"Good work, Mike. I'll be here most afternoons if you need any help on your speech."

"What speech?"

"You made salutatorian, my girl. You'll have five minutes at graduation to say whatever you want."

"Came in second, huh?"

Mike smiled and Mrs. Rook knew she was joking.

"Rich McKay beat you."

The guidance counselor ushered Mike into his office.

"Mike, I don't know how to tell you this."

The counselor played with the paper in his hand and Mike leaned forward in her seat.

46

"Go ahead and tell me. There's not much I can't handle anymore."

"Well, Mike. You still out on your own?"

Mike nodded.

"Any chance of living with your parents while you go to college?"

"Nope. They can't afford it and neither can I."

"I'm sorry to hear that. You see, there's a rule. Students under twenty-one can't live off campus unless they live with their family. And they also can't live on campus without parental consent. Do you think your parents would give their consent?"

Mike shook her head. Her dad might go along with it, but her mother would stop him. It wasn't that her mother wouldn't be proud of her for being a college graduate, but the mother-daughter problem had to be dealt with first. That would take a long time and different circumstances. Mike couldn't see any mending or healing in the near future.

"Any way you can give that scholarship to someone else?" Mike asked.

"Well, I suppose we could. If you're absolutely sure."

"I'm sure. Just don't tell whoever gets it that it was mine first, okay?"

❑ ❑

While waiting for her turn to speak, Mike scanned the crowd to see if anyone from her family was there.

"And the salutatorian for this year, with a grade point average of 3.96, ladies and gentlemen, Michaelene Landetti."

Mike could hear the "oohs" and "ahs" as she made her way to the rostrum. She didn't have a planned speech. She wanted to look out at the class she had returned to and let the words just come naturally.

"I suppose many of you are surprised to see me standing up here. I'm a little surprised myself. It took passing a lot of tests, being able to remember what my teachers said, and having a lot of time to think about things.

"It seems we all come to school on some kind of cloud, the same cloud we're born with. School is fun and friends, arguments and disappointments, ups and downs. Each day a little rain falls from that cloud until we reach our senior year, then there's just a little, tiny piece of cloud holding us up and keeping us going. Right behind that tiny cloud, is the sun. It might be college. It might be marriage. Or maybe it's just a good job. Whatever it is, we try to see it, try to reach out and grab it. Some people use other people's clouds to get there. Some people fall off, and keep on falling, never able to get back on the cloud or reach for that sun again. Well, I was lucky. My cloud was a little bigger than some of yours. It held a lot more tears. I almost jumped off and let myself fall as far as gravity would take me. But I was lucky. I had friends. People who cared. And all of you formed a rainbow behind me. A bridge to the sun. A path that may not lead me to college or marriage, or even a good job. But it'll lead me somewhere. And you can bet if any of you ever need me to hold you up or give you an extra push, I'll be right there on that rainbow you gave me, and I won't let you down. Thank you."

The crowd was silent except for a few sighs and some stifled sobs. Mike took her diploma from the principal and walked right out of the auditorium. She could hear the applause as she left. She left her cap and gown at the door and then made her way down Main Street, through the cemetery, up and around Newton Street, along Central Avenue, and into the Marine Corps recruitment office. Two weeks later, Mike was on a bus to Parris Island, South Carolina.

She'd stayed busy, making sure she made no good-byes. She wanted a clean break from everything and everyone. She sent a note to Gus so she'd know where she was, but this time, she made no promises and left no address.

❏ ❏

They arrived at four a.m., were in bed by four-thirty, and up again by a quarter to five. Mike didn't mind. She had chosen the Marines because they were supposed to be the toughest branch of the military. She thought she might even want to go to Vietnam and kill some of the people who had killed friends she'd grown up with. She hoped that the women Marines were as tough as the men and that they would all learn the same things.

"Where you from?" a tall, dark-haired woman whispered to Mike.

At first Mike didn't answer. The drill instructor had ordered no talking, and Mike wasn't about to get in trouble.

"Did you hear me? I asked where you're from?"

Mike stayed at attention.

"I'm from Huntsville, Alabama," one woman said.

"Keyport, New Jersey," said another.

Sergeant Morris came to the line and stood nose to nose with Mike.

"Did I hear talking coming from this line?"

Mike kept her eyes straight ahead.

"I'm talking to you, recruit. Were you talking in my line?"

"Yes, ma'am," Mike shouted.

"Did I tell you to talk in my line?"

"No, ma'am."

"Then why were you talking, recruit?"

"No excuse, ma'am."

Mike kept herself at rigid attention while Sergeant Morris eyed the women around her.

"You, you, and you. To the end of the line. I want ten push-ups from each of you and then report to my office."

Sergeant Morris had singled out all the talkers, but not Mike.

"You, Recruit Landetti, are a good Marine. If you other girls were half the Marine she already is, you wouldn't be in trouble. Landetti, you're the platoon leader from now on."

"Yes, ma'am."

Mike noticed a slight smile from Sergeant Morris.

"By the way, platoon leader. Where are you from?"

"A small town south of Buffalo, New York, ma'am."

"They have other Marines as good as you back home?"

"Not anymore, ma'am."

The days started early and ended late, but they weren't as hard as Mike had hoped. Women Marines were expected to wash, starch, and iron their own uniforms. The men sent theirs to the cleaners. Women Marines got rifle training only twice, and the obstacle course was "feminized" to suit the softer women. Even the military specialties were different for women. A woman couldn't be tested for combat, engineering, flying, or anything else that seemed too male.

When testing day came, Mike only saw one specialty that interested her: journalism. Being a military journalist could be exciting and might even get her to Vietnam. She made sure she did her best in journalism and failed every other test.

"Recruit Landetti reporting as ordered, ma'am."

Sergeant Morris ordered her at ease and spoke in a quiet voice.

"Landetti, tomorrow you graduate and become a full Marine. A private. Actually, you'll be one of two promoted to private first class."

"Thank you, ma'am."

"You did that yourself, Mike. You're the best damn recruit I think I've ever had. A little too friendly with the other girls sometimes, but a damn good Marine. That's why I wanted to tell you about your orders today. You didn't get journalism. They're sending you to electronics school."

"Ma'am? I don't understand."

"You got a 99 in journalism and a 61 in electronics. You're the first woman to ever score that high in electronics."

"Ma'am, I thought 61 was a failing score, ma'am."

"By every standard, it is. But the Corps wants to see how women do in electronics, and your score was high enough to make them think you can do it. After your leave, you'll report to San Diego."

Sergeant Morris shook Mike's hand.

"I'm sorry, Mike. I know what you wanted, and I think I know why. Just between you and me, I think you'll do just fine. We'll miss you around here."

Mike would miss Sergeant Morris, too. Morris was short and tough with a golden heart under her brass buttons.

Mike had two weeks' leave before her one-year electronics course began — and people she wanted to see.

❑ ❑

"I don't believe it!" Gus was cool when Mike showed up in her uniform. "You really did it! You went off and joined the Army!"

"Marines."

"What difference does it make? It still makes you a killer. Have you heard about the war? How about the peace movement? Anyone tell you about that?"

"I needed an education and a job, Gus. What's so bad about it?"

"Look at you in that monkey suit! The military is what's wrong. We got friends being drafted and dying and you go down and sign up?"

"I needed a job."

"Then go to work. I don't even want to look at you."

Mike couldn't believe Gus was talking to her like that. What was so bad about fighting for your country? She was proud to salute the flag. She was proud she had earned her stripe by being a good Marine.

She searched old hangouts for friends, but most people wouldn't even look at her. She walked through the cemetery and sat for a long time by the maple tree. She knew she was really saying good-bye: to her friends, her town, her past. She'd never be back. She silently forgave Gus. Her friend was just trying to protect herself in a world where "The Times They Are A-Changing."

MISSION HILL

San Diego was as beautiful as Mike had thought it would be: almost peaceful, with salty air that was different from that of the East Coast, and a sun that promised an end to cold winters. Her barracks was filled with a dozen women, two assigned to each cubicle. They marched to their schools at 4:30 a.m. and returned to homework and military duties at 5 p.m. Sundays, they had to themselves, and some Saturdays, unless the duty roster said it was your turn for fire watch or garden party. Fire watch was the hardest. Duty began at 8 p.m. and lasted until early morning. Mike walked the halls watching for fires and making bed checks on supposedly sober and sleeping Marines.

"Private Landetti, we'd like you to work for us. To be on our side, so to speak."

The man who spoke to her didn't give his name. He said only that he worked for Civilian Intelligence, a kind of nonmilitary CIA.

"We'd like you to keep an eye out for drugs, liquor, disobedience, that sort of thing. And then report back to us so we can take care of it. In return, you'll be given regular promotions, extra leave days, and, when you're done with training, a choice of duty stations."

"I don't think so, sir."

"Private, I don't think you understand. You don't really have the option of saying no."

He walked behind her and put a hand on her shoulder.

"Let me put it this way," he continued, "if you refuse, and I know you're smart enough to not refuse, life in the Marines could be very difficult for you. Understand?"

"No, sir." Mike maintained her stance and tried to relax her fists.

"Let me give you the bottom line, Private. We want the druggies, the drunks, the lesbos, and little bitches that fuck up. And we want you to help us find them. Do I make myself clear?"

"Very clear, sir."

"Well, then. We have a deal, right?"

"No, sir."

The man blew smoke in Mike's face and gritted his teeth.

"Then you're dismissed, Private. Oh, one more thing. One word about this to anyone and I'll bounce your sweet ass into the brig. Got it?"

"Yes, sir."

The next day's duty roster showed Mike on fire watch six weekends in a row.

Synde shook her head as she read the roster with Mike. Everyone called her Synde, but her real name was Gail-something. She had been close to Mike in boot camp and now shared her cubicle.

"Man, oh man, someone's got it in for you!"

"I suppose," Mike said. "Maybe after six weeks I won't get duty again for a year. Maybe that's just how they do it."

"First time I ever heard of it. I'll stay on base and keep you company if you want."

That weekend, a woman Mike didn't know remained on base and played her radio until all hours of the night. "House of the Rising Sun" seemed to be her favorite song. Though Mike was tired of hearing it, she left her alone.

Sunday, while Mike was making her usual rounds, the radio suddenly stopped. Finally, the woman must be sleeping, Mike decided, feeling glad for the quiet. Just before dawn, Mike greeted Synde at the door and walked her to their cubicle.

"Awful quiet around here," Synde said.

"It wasn't for a while. Someone had her radio blaring almost all weekend. The one at the end down there."

"Bet you're glad she left."

"I think she's still here. Just sleeping."

"Better check. It's almost time for everyone to be back and you have to do a bed check."

"You're right."

Mike walked into the cube at the end of the hall and found the woman asleep. She started to leave, but then noticed pills strewn all over the floor.

"Oh, shit! Synde! Get the duty officer! On the double!"

She heard Synde running down the hall and went over to the woman to see if she was alive or dead. Kneeling down beside her, Mike felt for a pulse. She wasn't sure if she could detect one, so she checked the woman's neck.

"Stay with me," the woman whispered. "Help me."

"You're alive. Shit, thank God."

"Sit with me. Don't leave." The woman clutched Mike's arm and pulled.

"Just take it easy," Mike said. "I'm right here. The duty officer's on her way. You'll be okay."

Mike turned toward the hallway and shouted, "Synde! Hurry up!"

"Stay with me. I'm dying. Sit with me."

"I'm right here."

Mike sat on the edge of the bed holding the woman's cold hand.

"Private Landetti. You're under arrest."

The company commander and two military policemen stood waiting at the cubicle door. Mike sprang to attention.

"Sir, what for, sir?"

"For attempted sodomy and influencing a minor. Take her away."

The MPs took Mike by the arms and dragged her out of the cubicle.

"Attempted sodomy? Are you crazy? This woman's dying! Can't you see she's dying?"

The woman propped herself up and smiled. "I feel fine," she said. "What were you doing on my bed?"

Mike was stunned.

"You set me up!" she screamed. "This is all a setup! Because I wouldn't play your stupid game?"

She kicked and fought as the MPs hauled her down the corridor. When Synde and a female officer moved out of their way, Mike glared at Synde like a madwoman.

"You helped them. You're on their side. I thought we were friends, and you helped them."

Synde had tears in her eyes and kept shaking her head, but Mike didn't believe she was innocent. She felt deceived and angry and wild. And she never wanted to trust anyone again.

They took her to Navy Psychiatric, where they guarded her until the doctor could arrive. One of the MPs sneered at her as he rocked back and forth in his spit-polished shoes.

"Don't worry, chicky. They'll have you tested and outta here on the next bus home. Marines don't like no lezzies on their team."

Mike didn't know what a lezzie was, but no one was sending her home. She readied herself on the end of her chair and waited until the guards relaxed their vigil. As soon as the time was right, she ran. She was fast: faster than they were and faster than anyone she knew. Running was a game to her, a sport, something she could do better than other people, something Coach Conway had appreciated. They blew their whistles and chased after her — past the mess hall, across the parade deck, beyond the electronics school to the airport gate. Five jeeps came at her from all directions. She took off her watch and threw it against the gate, jumping away when the sparks flew. She was trapped. A lone animal in a kingdom she didn't know. They put her in hand- and legcuffs and drove her back to the doctor.

"That's right, come right in and take a seat."

The doctor led her to a desk and asked the MPs to remove the cuffs.

"She's a runner, sir. Beat two of my best men in a footrace across the base."

"Is that so? I don't think she'll run anymore, will you, dear?"

Mike shrugged her shoulders in defiance and rubbed the welts on her wrists. If she knew where to run, she would. The doctor sat down across from her and shuffled some papers.

"So, you're a runner. You like to run?"

Mike nodded.

"Good, good. Proud of that ability, aren't you?"

Mike nodded again.

"Fine. We're doing just fine. Now then, what I'd like you to do is draw me a picture. I'm sure you like to draw. But this picture will be a very special one. I'd like you to draw your family for me. You know, just like in grade school? Mommy, Daddy, you, your house. Go ahead. Take your time."

Mike cracked her neck and picked up the pencil. This man was crazy, as crazy as she'd ever seen, but he was a captain and he held her future in his hairy hands.

She tried to determine the object of the picture drawing and decided it was a psychological trick. She was supposed to draw one figure larger than the other so they could diagnose her problem as one of dominance.

She carefully drew all the figures the appropriate size. Her father was almost six feet and her mother was five inches shorter. She put herself between them and the house behind the trio. The doctor studied the picture through his military glasses.

"I see. I see. Very good. Now I'm going to ask you a series of questions. I'd like you to answer as quickly as possible. Comprehend?"

"Misinterpret."

The doctor was annoyed at Mike's joke, but turned to his list and began his questions.

"Boys?"

"Girls."

"Very good, Private. Now, fill in the blank. Girls are blank."

"The opposite of boys."

"Mothers are blank."

"Also daughters."

"Sex is blank."

"Private."

"The Marine Corps is blank."

Mike stuck out her chest and sighed.

"Blood and guts," she said.

They continued the test for more than an hour. When it was over, Mike couldn't think of anything she'd said that wasn't normal, or at least normal for psychiatrists.

It was a sergeant, not the doctor, who finally came out of the office with her results.

"Let her go, men. This little lady has the only perfect score we've ever seen. She's no queer."

The sergeant smiled and gave her a pass to return to her barracks.

"You're free to go," he said.

"What about the charges? My record?"

"Just a mistake. Your duty officer will clear it all up."

Mike returned to a barracks full of whispers. She headed straight for the cubicle at the end of the hall.

"Where's the bitch who lived here?"

She searched the faces around her for an answer.

"Where is she?"

"She's gone, Private."

Lieutenant Mitchell, the duty officer, motioned for Mike to go to her own cubicle.

"We have some talking to do," she said.

"Yes, ma'am."

The lieutenant took a seat and gestured to Mike to do the same. She closed the cubicle curtain and pulled out a pipe and a tobacco pouch.

"I like to smoke to relax. Want some?"

Mike shook her head. She'd never seen a woman smoke a pipe.

"The way I see it," said Mitchell, "you got a bum rap. We all get lonely sometimes. All of us need a teddy bear once in a while. I don't see you being much different. They'll leave you alone now. For a while, anyway. But you have to be careful. If you get lonely, go off base and take care of it there. Don't mess around in the barracks."

"But the woman looked like she was dying. I wasn't sitting on her bed because I'm lonely."

"You were on her rack for some reason, Private. You know regulations. Even if she really was dying, you had no business sitting on her rack."

Mitchell puffed her pipe and then smiled at Mike.

"I know your DI from boot camp. Sergeant Morris. She says you're a good kid. Just take my advice. The next time, go off base."

She snuffed out her pipe and stood up. Mike stood at attention readying a salute.

"Relax, Private. This is informal. Just between you and me. Same with the pipe. Just between you and me."

After Mitchell patted Mike's shoulder and left, Mike slumped to her bed in exhaustion. Tentatively, Synde came in and took Mitchell's vacated seat.

"It wasn't me, Mike. I'd never do anything like that. Not to you, or anyone."

Mike studied her eyes for truth and, wordlessly, turned facedown on her bed.

"Mike, tell me you believe me. I'd never hurt you like that."

"I believe you."

❏ ❏

Synde finished her school in twelve weeks and got orders to ship out to Camp Twenty-Nine Palms.

"I have something for you," she said to Mike.

Mike had kept her distance from everyone and acted detached with Synde.

"It's half a St. Jude medal. I want you to wear it. If you ever need me, or get in trouble, send it to me."

She stood very close to Mike and put the medal on a chain and the chain over Mike's head. Mike checked to make sure the curtain was closed. She recognized the look in Synde's eyes and didn't want any part of it.

"I'll send you mine if you send me yours," Mike said.

"That's a deal," Synde said, and kissed Mike's cheek.

Electronics school got harder and harder. Being the only woman isolated Mike. Though she didn't get the same support as the men, she was determined to make it through. At first, the male Marines were put off by her. They believed the school should be for men only and felt inhibited by her presence. But the service is full of camaraderie and it wasn't long before Mike was invited to the same parties and bars. She willingly went along. It was easy being with them and reminded her of her days with Steve and Hank.

The one thing their instructor had told them on the first day was to stay away from Tijuana, Mexico. Of course, telling them to stay away from something was an invitation to disaster. At their first chance, Mike and six male buddies hopped a bus for TJ.

The streets were lined with filth and strip shows and street hawkers trying to sell everything from rotten beer to their virgin sisters.

"Come in, come in. One dollar for the best ass in town."

"No, no, *señors*. This way. The girls are here waiting for you."

One hawker caught Mike's arm and tried to persuade her to enter his shack.

"Come in. Please. Tits and ass for sale here."

Mike jerked her arm away. "I'm a girl, asshole."

"Ah. A lesbian. Come. The girls will like you."

Mike joined her friends at a more reasonable bar where they chugged beer until morning.

The next day, Mike awoke with a terrible headache and a swollen ankle. She couldn't remember twisting or hurting it in any way, and it didn't feel like a normal sprain. Monday, she marched to school as usual, but her foot and ankle were turning blue and the pain was excruciating.

By the end of the week, her whole leg was blue, and Mike decided it was time for sick bay.

The hall was full of Marines, some very sick, others obviously faking it to get out of something. The doctor left the examining room door wide open. A flimsy curtain near the examination table provided the only privacy. Mike was glad only her leg needed checking. She could roll up her utility pants and still maintain her dignity.

The doctor took all the information about her leg and made some notes in her file.

"Up here and remove your clothing, please."

"Sir?"

"Remove your clothing."

"But you're only looking at my leg. Why do I have to get undressed?"

"All females automatically get a gynecological exam when they report to sick bay."

Mike was astounded. They weren't going to get her on any table where she could be pawed and peered at.

"Forget it," she said. "It'll heal."

"Suit yourself," said the doctor. "But I'll have to make an entry that you refused treatment."

"Enter what you want. The only thing I refused was clinical rape."

Her leg continued to swell and turn colors, and soon the other one followed. Mike tied her oxfords as tightly as possible so that she could walk around the base. But by the time she returned to the barracks, she found it too painful to stand, and people had to carry her from place to place. After eleven days, she got on a bus and went to Balboa Naval Hospital.

"Emergency! Emergency! Vehicular accident case!"

"No, sir," Mike interrupted. "They've been like this for almost two weeks."

"My God, Private. You look like you've been crushed by a car."

"It kinda feels that way, sir."

They put her in a ward and raised the foot of her bed. Every hour, they came to take blood or urine. Mike felt relieved and exhausted. She had fought the pain for too long and now it had caught up with her. For three days, she writhed and screamed at the piercing needles in her legs. And she worried about school. No one was allowed to miss more than seven days. It meant a desk job, and she didn't want that.

White nodules began appearing on both legs and Mike became the object of medical wonder. Every day, more doctors examined her and took new tests. When her school commander visited, Mike knew it was bad news.

"Private. How are you feeling?"

"Fine, sir. I'll be up in no time."

The major smiled and patted her sore leg.

"I see. We have a problem, Private."

"No problem, sir. I can still study. Someone's going to bring me the notes and ... and I'm getting more books so I'll understand the projects."

"How would you like to go to OCS, Private?"

"Officer's Candidate School, sir?"

"Yes. I think you'd be a good one. I understand you walked and marched on those legs for two weeks, is that right?"

"Yes, sir. But I wouldn't do it again. I'd be more careful next time."

"You don't understand. I admire your courage. Your perseverance in the face of pain. The doctors tell me you almost lost those legs."

Mike closed her eyes in shock. She hadn't thought it was that bad.

"I know men who couldn't do what you did. You'd make a fine leader in the Marine Corps."

"What about school, sir?"

"Is it really important for you to finish this electronics thing?"

"Yes, sir."

61

"Then you will. I'll fix it with your instructor. When school's done, I want an answer on OCS."

"Yes, sir."

The major saluted and Mike returned it.

❏ ❏

"Are you the one they call Mike?"

Mike opened her eyes to a beautiful smiling face.

"I'm Sue. Corporal Weathers. Are you Lance Corporal Landetti?"

"I'm Landetti, but I'm just a PFC."

"Not anymore. Your promotion came while you were sleeping. Twenty-eight more dollars a month."

Mike dragged herself to a sitting position and covered her legs so Sue wouldn't see them.

"Do they know what's wrong yet?" Sue asked.

"No. They think it's some kind of blood poisoning, but they're not sure. They've never seen it before. Probably got it in TJ." Mike thought of the morning the doctors had told her she might never walk again. Turning from Sue, she shyly wiped away her tears.

"Funny. People always say when you're a runner, the legs are the first to go."

Sue sat next to the bed and gently rubbed Mike's shoulder.

"You should go ahead and cry. Sometimes crying makes you stronger."

Sue's gentle touch and the thought of someone caring made it almost impossible for Mike to control her tears. But she held them in. She didn't know who this girl was or what she wanted, but she wasn't going to cry in front of her.

"Major Todd says I should keep you company and help you study. Then, after this thing clears up, I'll be your rehab nurse."

Mike and Sue spent days together trying to understand capacitance and resistance and Ohm's law. After seven weeks, the nodules on Mike's legs began to disappear and the color was returning to normal. It was no longer as painful to sit up and dangle her legs and, with a little help, she could make it to the shower.

Sue helped her into a wheelchair and, despite Mike's protests that her arms were fine, insisted on rolling her to the bathroom.

"Uh, it's time for you to turn around so I can get undressed."

Sue smiled and turned her back. "I keep forgetting your shyness."

"I never could get undressed in front of anybody," Mike said.

She unbuttoned the hospital shirt and pulled it over her head.

"People in school used to think I was pretty weird. I'd always wait until everyone else was done with their showers, then I'd go in. I was the fastest shower taker you ever saw! Oh, shit!"

Mike's right leg buckled, forcing her to the shower floor. Sue quickly grabbed her to help her back into the chair, but the floor was slippery, and Mike was heavy.

"I can do it. I can do it!"

"Sure you can do it. That's why you're on the floor. Give me your arm."

Sue put Mike's arm over her shoulder. Mike could smell her and feel her warmth.

"Put your weight on your left leg. It's stronger than the right. That's it. Now see if you can push on it to stand."

Mike pushed, holding on to Sue and the wall. She was almost upright when she slipped again. Sue caught her. Mike's bare breasts brushed against Sue's body; she put her hands on Sue's waist to balance herself. She was embarrassed and could feel the heat rise in her face, but Sue didn't move. Mike tried to avoid her eyes and move back toward the chair but Sue held fast.

"I really need to sit—"

"No you don't. I can hold you."

"But it's kind of hard to—"

"Can't you for once just shut up."

63

Mike looked at her face and then darted her eyes toward the shower room door.

"There's no one else scheduled. It's just you and me."

Sue gently pulled her closer. They kissed with a deepness Mike had forgotten. It was one of those kisses that never stops, never needs air.

Sue drew the curtain on the shower stall and pushed Mike into her chair. Then she started taking off her clothes. "I want you. From the first time I saw you, I've wanted you."

"Not here," Mike said. "We can't do this here."

"I'm your therapist. No one will know."

Panic surged through Mike as she watched Sue undress. She had never been this close to a naked woman. Sharon had always kept her clothes on. Gus never took off her nightgown. Even her cousin wore pajamas on their make-believe dates.

Sue straddled Mike's lap and leaned to kiss her again. Mike could feel her breasts pressing up against her own. She could feel Sue's softness, the bones in her back, the sucking wetness inside her mouth.

"Make love to me."

Sue moved up and down on Mike's lap and Mike let her inner sense take over so she could please her. She listened to her breathing, felt Sue's warm breath mix with her own. She moved her head and tongue down Sue's body and savored her taste. She gently sucked the rigid nipples, then moved her tongue in a flutter across the tips.

"Oh, God. You're such a good lover. Even like this, you're so good. I knew you would be. I knew you'd know how to love me. Oh, Mike. Hold me. Hold me tight. You're mine now. You're mine. Hold me. Love me. Don't let go. Don't stop. Don't stop!"

Mike moved her hand and her fingers. Slowly. Then quickly. Then slowly again. She licked and sucked and tasted and smelled and savored every part of Sue she could reach.

Finally, Sue arched, pressing Mike's face into her chest. Mike felt the warm wetness ooze from Sue's body as Sue slumped into her arms. For minutes, hours, what seemed like days, they sat in the shower stall holding each other. Mike watched as the beautiful woman who had made her a lover fell asleep in her arms.

❏ ❏

Mike walked better every day. The doctors said it was an amazing recovery. They still didn't know the cause, and they hadn't found a cure, but Mike was walking and Sue was walking close beside. Sue scheduled Mike for physical therapy three times a day. Though Mike was usually tired by the third session, she knew the appointments were planned so that she and Sue could be alone in the therapy room. They hadn't dared make love again after the risky first time, but for twelve weeks they kissed and laughed and worked together to make Mike well.

"I guess I'm getting out of here tomorrow."

"I'm afraid of that. I know you have to go, but I'm afraid."

"I'll still see you on weekends, and some nights."

"It won't be the same. Things will change."

Mike made sure no one was watching, then took Sue's hand and led her to the weight room. She pretended to lift weights with her right leg while she held Sue's hand close to her heart.

"Everything changes. People change. But we can change together. We'll find a way."

"The base is a long way from here."

"So we'll buy a car. Or take a bus. It won't matter. It won't be the same, but it won't matter. I'm not going anywhere."

"What about OCS?"

"I'm not going. I'd rather stay with the working slobs anyway. Officers are crazy. And lifers."

"You don't plan on staying in?"

"Not after my time is up. Too many phony rules and assholes."

"I didn't know you felt that way. Maybe there's a lot I don't know."

"Look, you're thinking about things the wrong way. Being a lifer wouldn't make me like you any more than I already do. It wouldn't keep me crippled so that nothing could change. Being a lifer would only give me orders to somewhere else."

Mike stopped the leglifts and pulled Sue close to her.

"We'll be together every time we can, every minute. I'll get a motel room and we'll spend the whole weekend making love. We'll go to Mission Hill, to a special place we'll make our own, and I'll love you in the pine forest. We'll be fine."

Two weeks later, Sue got orders for Vietnam: they needed a therapist for wounded Marines. Her work with Mike gave her a promotion and a new base. Sue called on the phone and Mike ran to catch the nearest bus. Hospital buses didn't operate as often as other buses. The only chance she had was a bus on the other side of the base. She raced along the same path she had used before: past the mess hall, across the parade deck. Her knees hurt and then buckled, driving her to the scraping ground. She tried to get up, but her knees were swelling from the strain. She tried to drag herself across the deck; the bus stop was only a football field away. She pulled and crawled and cried into the blacktop.

Weeks later, the swelling in her knees went down. Sixteen aspirin a day helped relieve the inflammation. Mike sat on Mission Hill, looking out over the city and the ocean. The Old Town lights were beneath her and lovers occasionally walked by without noticing her. "Leaving on a Jet Plane" played somewhere in the trees. The letter said Sue had been killed by a booby trap strapped to a little girl who had lost her leg to a shell. Sue had tried to help her into the hospital. The shelling was far away. There was no danger. But when Sue had picked up the little girl, she'd been blown to pieces. In her gear was a letter addressed to Mike. A letter that said she'd be back. That they'd meet on the hill, in their special spot, and nothing would change.

GUITAR
MAMA

Mike didn't finish electronics school at the top of her class. In fact, she barely finished at all. Nothing interested her, nothing excited her. She didn't care about winning or competing or ever being anything. Friends told her she needed to forgive herself and move on, that Sue was just a friend caught in the storm like so many others. Lieutenant Mitchell tried to help by driving Mike around San Diego, taking her to beaches, parks, and the zoo, but Mike couldn't forget. She hated the war, the Marines, and any God who allowed death and destruction. Lieutenant Mitchell cut Mike's orders to Camp Pendleton and drove her up the coast to her new barracks. Mike was a radio technician now, in charge of teaching male Marines the tricks of the trade. Camp Pendleton had more than 40,000 Marines; only 128 of them were women. It was a sprawling desert base surrounded by mountains and howling coyotes. The women's barracks was a new structure built close to the ground, with three floors and two to a room. Mike got a room to herself with a blue door and a promotion to corporal. She was made barracks NCO almost immediately, which made her responsible for just about everything and everybody there.

The barracks lounge was built mainly to receive male visitors, but a pool table and piano kept the women occupied when they weren't interested in men or bars.

Mike's radio shack was a ten-minute ride by military cab. She made the trip every morning at ten to eight and returned every night at ten after five. Every day, she got the same cabdriver, a Southern guy with a Rebel flag in the window and an accent that wouldn't quit.

"How ya doin' today, Corporal? This here Marine Corps still givin' you a hard time?"

Mike always responded with the same Southern accent. It was a game that made the driver friendly and it helped her smile before she had to face her male students' egos.

"Same as always there, Frank. Same as always."

"Back home we'd be kickin' some ass if someone pulled shit on us, ain't that right?"

"Sure is. Ain't no boys I know ever put up with this."

"Hee, you are right there. We got some good ol' boys for sure. Where 'bouts you from again?"

"The South, same as you."

"But what parts? Sure do sound like a Virginia accent to me."

"Born in Jamestown, you sure are right."

"Jamestown, huh? Jamestown, Virginia. There's a lot of good ol' boys up that way."

The days never seemed to change. Mike was always getting reprimanded by her sergeant for not paying attention. She put up with it for six months, then started going to sick bay complaining about anything she could think of. A friendly nurse always let her off the hook, putting her on light duty so she didn't have to go right back to work. But each time she returned to the radio shack, her sergeant was madder; each time, she came closer to losing her job.

On the days she stayed in the barracks, she practiced pool and the piano, got her lunch from something called the "roach coach" that pulled up outside, and waited for people to get out of work so she'd have someone to talk to.

Christmas was the loneliest time. Only Mike and a handful of others had no home to go to, so they stayed in the barracks and shared cookies and music and dirty jokes. "Blue Christmas" played over and over. Even Brenda Lee's Christmas tree couldn't help them feel very jolly. Mike changed the record to the Rolling Stones and they all sang as loud as they could.

> *We gotta get out of this place,*
> *If it's the last thing we ever do.*
> *We gotta get out of this place.*
> *Girl, there's a better life, for me and you.*

"Hey, Mike. There's a corporal down the hall who wants to see the barracks NCO."

"Tell her to come out to the lounge with everyone else."

"She says you gotta go there. She don't like all the noise out here."

Mike knocked loudly on the door and heard a very faint "Come in."

"Yank says you have some kind of problem?"

"I just don't like the noise, that's all. I don't mind the singing, but I'm working. Isn't there any way you could hold it down?"

"It's Christmas, for Christ's sake. These people have to let off a little steam so they don't go out and kill themselves."

"Is that your job? To make sure people don't kill themselves?"

"Sometimes. I guess it is. I have people in my office sometimes ready to go crazy. They come to me first, drunk and sober, looking for a way to end all the craziness."

"And you provide the magic cure?"

"In a way. Sometimes I hand them a baseball bat and let them have at it on cardboard boxes. They come out sweaty and crying and exhausted, but they're alive."

"Look, I've heard how good you are at calming things down, but I live here, too. I just want it a little quieter so I can play my guitar. That's how I stay alive."

"All right. That's cool. I can understand that. What kind of stuff do you play?"

"Folk. And classical. But I don't suppose you'd know what that means."

"Just stay there, lady. I'll be right back."

As Mike ran through the lounge, she asked Yank to turn down the record player.

"We're going to be doin' some serious jammin' in 101 so you gotta keep it down."

She rushed back to 101, guitar in hand, and put one foot on the bed for balance.

"I'm ready when you are. What's your name?"

"Loren. How about something a little warmer than the usual Christmas songs?"

She plucked and Mike strummed and together they sang "Summertime."

"You're pretty good," Mike said when they ended.

Laughter and clapping rang through the halls behind Mike. She turned to bow to the lounge group.

"Thank you. Thank you."

"I think I'd rather play alone." Loren put her guitar on the bed and held the door for Mike.

"What's wrong? They can leave if it bothers you."

"I just want to be alone."

She closed the door and Mike heard the lock click behind her.

The next day, Mike wrapped a tiny bow on a guitar pick and typed out a note on her office typewriter telling Loren she was sorry. She knocked on 101 and then slid the present under the door. Loren swung open the door immediately and caught Mike sneaking back down the hall.

"Come on in."

Putting on her best face, Mike cautiously walked into Loren's room. Loren unwrapped the pick and read the note with a smile.

"I really am sorry," Mike said. "I'm not usually like I was last night. They make me get a little cocky sometimes and I always feel bad afterward."

"Cocky is an understatement. Why are you so friendly with all of them? I don't think you're like them at all."

"I'm like them. We're here, with no way out and no where to go and no one who gives a damn. I'm like them."

"I heard you're smart," Loren said. "And you can do almost anything."

"They're all smart. Or just as dumb as you and I. You're here. Playing a guitar and singing to yourself to keep going. They're doing the same thing in their own way."

"But I'm in data processing. I want to make a career of it."

"Then you're just luckier than most. You got something you wanted and you like it. You're just luckier, not better."

"I was wrong about you. I think you'd better leave."

Mike didn't budge. "How come every time someone says something you don't like you tell them to leave? Look, we have to be like family here. No one can make it alone."

"I'll make it. Without your help."

"I hope you never eat those words."

The New Year's ruckus was worse than Christmas. There were more people on base, many were drinking, some smoked marijuana, and a few used LSD. The barracks was the noisiest it had ever been. Mike stayed sober, as usual, and helped people up the stairs or to their rooms. She stopped a fight between a black woman and a white woman by holding them both against the wall and kicking away the broken bottles. Black power didn't scare her; neither did white hate. She helped the women to their rooms, making sure they were both calm.

"Mike! Bring your keys! Something's happening in 101!"

Mike raced down the stairs and up the hall to Loren's room.

"Somebody help me!" Loren screamed.

Mike fumbled for the master key, but couldn't get the door unlocked. Others gathered in the hall, watching Mike crash her shoulder against the door.

"Shit. They jammed the lock!"

She ran to the exit and grabbed the fire extinguisher. Using it like a club, she smashed it again and again against the doorknob until it finally broke loose. The door swung open, and a man with a knife turned to face Mike. Without thinking, Mike slammed the extinguisher into his face. His teeth bounced off the wall and the knife flew from his hand. As Mike readied another blow, the man spun to the window and tried to climb out. Mike grabbed him by his feet to try and pull him back in, but he was too big. He slipped into the darkness.

She turned to Loren, who was shaking violently. The sheets were full of blood. Mike went to close the door.

"Someone call an ambulance. And the MPs."

She returned to Loren's bed and sat down next to her. Loren pulled away in terror, flailing her arms in the air.

"Shh. It's okay. He's gone. Shh. You're all right now. You'll be okay. He's gone. You're all right. Shh."

Using the sheet, Mike blotted the blood from Loren's hands and face. The rapist had used his knife to carve initials in her body. Through the blood, Mike could see the letters *U*, *S*, and *M*. She knew what the next letter was, and she didn't want to see where he'd carved it.

"Don't let him near me. Help me. Help me!"

"Shh. He's gone. It's me. Mike. I'm right here."

Loren blinked, as if seeing Mike for the first time, then jerked herself up and hugged Mike with all the life left in her. Mike held her and calmed her until the ambulance arrived.

"Watch the barracks, Yank. I'm going to the hospital with her. Tell the MPs they're looking for a guy with three teeth missing and a bloody nose. He'll probably show up at sick bay claiming he was in a fight. Tell them the guy used a knife and it looks like rape, but keep it quiet. She doesn't need the whole world knowing what happened."

Mike rode in the ambulance as close to Loren as she could. She felt responsible. If she had been watching the barracks like she was supposed to, instead of helping drunks to their rooms, maybe she would have caught the guy before he got in.

"Fifth attack this month, isn't it?" the attendant asked.

"Yeah, but we got the other ones before they could do any damage. Pretty dumb way to build a women's barracks. Out in the middle of nowhere, with easy access to the first floor and no security. Real smart."

Loren reached for Mike's hand and held it close to her cheek.

"Don't let anyone touch me. Help me."

"No one's gonna touch you. The doctors will fix you up and you'll be fine."

"Did you kill him? That man?"

"I wish."

Mike waited outside while the doctors examined and stitched, and then called the duty officer to let her know what had happened.

"Why are you there, Corporal? You're on duty here. Why are you there?"

"Because you're not, ma'am."

She slammed down the phone and continued her vigil.

"Who's this Mike she keeps asking for. Her boyfriend?"

"No. It's me. A nickname."

"Oh. Well, she's all stitched and pretty shaken up. We didn't find any evidence of semen, but we think there was penetration. She wants you to take her back to the barracks. She says she's afraid of the orderlies and doctors."

"I'll take her."

"Be forewarned. She's reacting very violently. I could hardly touch her. We gave her a sedative to calm her down, but she may try to strike out at you."

"I'm not a man, Doc."

Mike carried Loren to her room and sat with her through the night. Each time Loren awoke screaming or thrashing, Mike gently rocked her until she slept again.

By morning, Loren was awake and asking for water. Mike ran to the fountain with her cup. Putting an arm behind Loren to hold her up, Mike fed her sips of water.

"Pretty rough night, huh?" Mike sat on the edge of the bed and let Loren lean against her.

"I don't know what would have happened if you weren't there. He might have ... might have..."

She started crying, and Mike petted and soothed her.

"He might have. But he didn't. I'm having your room moved upstairs, and me and the captain are going to come to blows about putting security on the windows."

Loren sobbed in Mike's arms, slept, and sobbed some more. Mike spent most of January checking on her. By February, she'd won the battle to have bars put on the lower windows.

Loren's stitches scabbed and healed, but without plastic surgery, she'd always have the initialed scars. The rapist was caught and convicted, but only got six months in the brig. They shipped him off to 'Nam after that. No one ever heard from him again.

Mike spent so much time with Loren that she lost her job at the radio shack. They moved her to a warehouse to work with a woman named Laurie. Together, they dozed away the hours until quitting time. Laurie was red-haired, bright, and fun. Mike almost looked forward to work just to be near her. They found a black Labrador puppy roaming the hills near the warehouse and gave it a home in the upper loft. Sometimes, they stopped at the clubs on base to have a beer and listen to country music, and sometimes, they got drunk and walked arm in arm back to the barracks.

Each time she returned home, Mike checked on Loren. Loren usually wanted to talk or lay her head in Mike's lap so Mike could soothe her with her voice. Mike still felt responsible but, though she liked Loren and enjoyed helping her feel better, she preferred being with Laurie. By midsummer, Mike had started skipping days with Loren. She always got yelled at or a cold shoulder the following day.

"I hear you and Laurie are always out together," Loren said. "Someone told me you even have a puppy that you share."

"Big deal. We're good friends. And the puppy's cute as hell."

"Sounds a little weird, if you ask me."

"No weirder than you sleeping in my lap or asking me to rub your back to put you to sleep."

"Do you rub her back, too?"

"None of your business."

"She's pregnant, you know."

Dumbfounded, Mike stepped back. Laurie hadn't said anything about being pregnant.

"Where'd you hear that?"

"So, you didn't know. Everyone else does. Some Hawaiian guy's the father. She's keeping it hidden so the Marine Corps will have to support the baby."

"That's bullshit! Plain bullshit!"

Mike slammed Loren's door and went straight to Laurie's room.

"Someone told me you're pregnant and I wanna hear from you that you're not."

"Shh." After closing the door, Laurie placed Mike's hand on her belly.

"Feel. I thought I felt it kick."

"Laurie! Why? Why didn't you tell me? Why are you pregnant?"

Laurie kept her voice calm and reassuring.

"I didn't tell you because I didn't want to hurt you. I know how you feel about me."

"How I feel about you? How? How do I feel about you?"

Laurie spoke almost nonchalantly.

"You love me. Plain and simple. Same as you did Sue, except you never admitted it. I could tell. No one talks about someone like that when you're just friends. You loved her. And now you love me. And I didn't want to hurt you. So I didn't tell you."

Mike went to the window to avoid Laurie's eyes. She hadn't realized she loved her, but Laurie was right. She felt jealous and deceived.

"Whose baby is it?"

"You don't know him. And I don't want you to. A few months from now I'll be out of here with a ticket to Hawaii."

"When were you going to tell me?"

"When you asked. As close as we've been lately and as much as we've been touching each other, I figured we'd get around to sleeping together and you'd ask about my stomach."

"What the hell! What do you think I am? Some kind of toy?"

Mike felt Laurie's words tear through her insides and she couldn't stand being near her. She pushed by her gently and left without another word. She spent the rest of the day in her office wondering why women did things the way they did. Pregnancy was a way out. Better than drugs or suicide. Laurie would get a general discharge and live happily ever after with a Hawaiian. It didn't seem fair, and it didn't seem right, but it was real.

She crept into Laurie's room just after midnight and quietly knelt beside her bed. Slowly, she touched Laurie's stomach. Laurie held Mike's hand warmly against her.

"Come on," she whispered. "Climb in beside me and hold me around my stomach."

Laurie rolled to face the wall as Mike cozied up beside her.

"It's okay. Get closer. Let me mold right into you."

Mike pulled herself closer and rubbed the rounded stomach through the night. It wasn't her baby, and she was losing Laurie to a man she didn't know, but for now, she'd love her and warm her in the night and be the best friend she knew how to be.

INVESTIGATION

"**N**ame?"

"Landetti, sir."

"And your rank?"

"Sergeant."

"Sergeant?" While the major checked the file in front of him, Mike stayed at attention, eyeing the other officers in the room. Their faces told her something bad was going on. The lone woman, a lieutenant, seemed the angriest. Though her glare was full of hatred and disgust, Mike detected a degree of excitement in her gestures, like a hunter who couldn't wait for the kill.

"Says here you're a corporal, Landetti. Are you trying to impersonate a sergeant?"

"No, sir. I was promoted yesterday. Because of the fire, I think."

"The fire?" The major looked at his cohorts, who shrugged and checked their papers. He moved his face within an inch of Mike's.

"Are you telling me you started a fire and got promoted? Is that it, Landetti?"

"No, sir. I put it out."

The woman lieutenant stepped forward, but the major maintained his stance.

"There was a fire," the lieutenant said. "In the barracks. A fairly large one that started on a bulletin board and spread through the first floor. My records indicate, however, that the fire company extinguished the blaze. All women Marines had been evacuated from the premises."

Mike stayed silent. She couldn't defend herself unless asked a direct question. They could check with her company commander or the duty officer. The fire had been set on a bulletin board by someone who could no longer cope with the military. At first Mike went to the exits as if it were one of the many drills Marines robotically obeyed. The flames were near the exit door and Mike saw the extinguisher hanging on the wall. Her instincts sent her back into the smoke. Others choked and gagged as they made their way out to the mess hall hill and waited for the fire trucks. Mike felt the smoke grabbing at her tongue and strangling the muscles in her throat, but she continued spraying the flames until there was nothing but ash.

Once she was certain the fire was out, she stumbled to the lounge stairway to help two women on crutches escape the smoke-filled barracks. When the firemen finally arrived, she pointed them to the fire area and then collapsed on the grass, choking until she felt as if her tongue had been ripped from its roots. She shuddered as she remembered the fear that had overcome her once it was over.

"We want you to talk to us, Landetti. Captain Sims here is a lawyer. Not yours, ours. Lieutenant Marshall works for us in the provost's office. You may know Miss — I mean, Lieutenant — Prior, special investigator with Intelligence. Have a seat."

The major pointed to a straight-backed chair surrounded by bright lights. Mike squinted and slumped to avoid the glare, but officers redirected the lights with her every move.

"Now, we would appreciate truthful answers to our questions. Answers that may save you from a bad conduct discharge or a trip to the brig. That's right, Landetti, the brig. While we have you here, there are special investigators searching your room and the rooms of others like you. We're going to find out, whether you tell us or not. Make it easy on yourself. If you talk we might let you go. All we want is names."

Mike tried to find the major's face so she could show him her defiance, but all she could see were the silhouettes of whispering and plotting heads. She tried to picture her room, to think of anything incriminating they might find. They could get her on the jeans. Women were not allowed to wear them. She'd say they belonged to her boyfriend in 'Nam. The box of unopened kitchen knives under her bed were harmless enough. After all, she was a short-timer, out in six months, and she needed civilian things to start over again. The only other thing they might find suspicious was the lock on her door. It was taped open so that anyone and everyone could come to her when they needed her.

She felt reasonably safe. Others had drugs and booze and pictures and letters. Letters! There was one letter she had written Loren to make up with her after Laurie had left for Hawaii. But it wasn't very mushy, and Loren's room probably wouldn't be searched. She was too straitlaced, too eager to do anything anyone told her, too willing to obey to get another stripe.

Mike's anger boiled as she waited for questions she knew she wouldn't answer. She was invaded, at war. The Marine Corps had trained her to fight the enemy, trained her for interrogation in case of capture. She was ready. The eagle, globe, and anchor on her hat, what men call a "piss-cover," dug into her forehead as she glared at her captors.

The major bent forward. "Who's your girlfriend, Landetti?" he sneered. "How many are there? How many do you have?"

He snickered while waiting for Mike's answer.

"Landetti, Michaelene. Sergeant. W721907."

"What the hell is this? I asked you a question, Marine! This isn't a goddam game. You're going to get booted out of here, you understand that? We know about you. We've heard about your lesbian antics, your drinking and drug taking. We know! We're trying to help you, give you a break, maybe give you a general discharge that won't hurt you so much."

He whispered with the others, then leaned forward with a smile.

"Do yourself a favor," he said. "We've got you. Just tell us who else and make it easier on yourself. They sure as hell told on you, and we'll find more who'll give us your name. You help us, and maybe we'll help you."

Fear clouded Mike's thoughts. They could put her in jail. After all, wasn't her love illegal? But they couldn't really know, could they? Who would tell? If they really had her, she could get out and be done with them. All they wanted was a few names. Mike knew every one of the 138 women in the barracks, and some of them she hated. Names could be easy.

"Sir, I don't know any names."

"Oh, for Christ's sake."

The major pushed his chair back in disgust.

"This woman is dumber than I thought," he said.

They whispered, wrote notes, and whispered some more.

"You're dismissed, Landetti. But we'll see you again. I promise you, we'll see you again. Now get out of our sight!"

Mike stood to attention, turned on her heel, and made sure the door slammed just a little as she left. She went directly to her room to check the damage.

❑ ❑

"Word is it's an all-out witch-hunt," Yank said.

Mike turned to acknowledge her in the doorway, then continued folding her clothes.

"Holy shit! They really tore this place apart," said Yank. "What the hell they got against you?"

She helped Mike pick up papers and clothes strewn across the room. The mattresses were tipped against the wall and the bed frame dismantled. All the drawers were emptied onto the floor and the closet and shelves were ransacked.

"Heard they're trying to clear out the ranks. They wanna make room for a bunch of guys comin' back from 'Nam. Too many promotions over there and too many women corporals and sergeants over here. They're callin' in everybody. The whole barracks is getting the third degree. It's nuts, Mike. You know?"

"Have you been in yet?"

Yank shook her head. "Nope. They got my room, but I've been kinda hiding out, avoiding everybody."

"Well, you're here. They've seen you with me. It won't be long now, I guess."

They stacked papers and put the bed back together. When the room was almost inspection-ready, Yank put her hand on Mike's shoulder.

"You oughtta punch that bitch right in the mouth," she said.

"The lieutenant?"

"No. Loren. She's the one who turned you in. They called her in right after you left. She gave them a letter and a note you wrote. They were gushing over her, patting her on the back. You really oughtta bash her!"

Mike waited until after dinner, when most people, including the investigators, were off duty, and then went to Loren's room. She took a deep breath before knocking on the door the way she did almost every day.

"Who is it?" Loren called from inside.

"Just me."

The long silence convinced Mike that Yank was telling the truth. When Loren finally opened the door, Mike held back her anger.

"Just wanted to tell you there's an investigation going on. They'll probably get around to calling you in. They'll make you all kinds of promises — you know, promotions, choice of duty station, things like that. The best thing to do is to keep quiet. They're tricky, you know. They'll make you tell 'em something that may only be half-true, and you'll think you're off the hook; then they'll get your name from someone and turn everything back on you. Best thing to say is nothing. For your own good."

Mike wanted to cry as she watched Loren avoid her eyes. Yank was right.

"The thing is," Mike continued, "they think we're dumb enough to believe them. As if any of us would screw over another woman Marine. Almost funny, isn't it?"

Loren kept her eyes down and slowly closed the door. "I have to go," she said. "I've had a bad day."

❏ ❏

All through the following day, Mike watched as one woman after another was called into the interrogation room. Most seemed like little children going in to be punished by a parent — afraid, but dutiful. Mike tried to give each one a thumbs-up sign, to give them some strength to resist, but many came out with their heads bowed and spirits broken.

By late afternoon, Mike gave up her post and went to her room. A four-day weekend was coming and she just wanted to get off base and be by herself. At four p.m., the loudspeaker blared through the barracks.

"Inspection in fifteen minutes. Full-dress greens in front of the barracks. Inspection, ladies."

Mike heard the groans through the halls as she quickly changed into her ever-ready inspection clothes.

They fell in outside and stood at attention while a very fat man smelling of garlic and beer and wearing stains on his shirt like combat ribbons inspected each woman from head to toe. Camp Pendleton's temperature was 96 degrees and the long inspection began to take its toll. Women swooned in the heat and shook from fear. When one woman fainted, Mike broke ranks to carry her to a couch in the lounge. The inspecting officer looked at her, but didn't stop her. Mike fanned the woman until she was conscious.

"Stay in here," she said. "That guy'll never miss ya."

But Mike returned to her position. Some women swayed and a few went to their knees.

"Landetti, isn't it?"

"Yes, sir."

"You have a smudge on your shoe, Sergeant. Three points off. Maybe next time you'll let the girls take care of themselves. Breaking ranks cost you."

At five-thirty the inspection was over and the bad news came from the company commander.

"Well, ladies, you failed. My orders are to confine you all to the barracks until further notice. As of now, all areas outside the barracks are off-limits. Have a nice holiday, ladies."

An angry silence filled the halls as people returned to their rooms. Mike glared at Loren as she entered her room. She wanted her to feel more than just her stare.

Yank sat on a chair near Mike's desk.

"Man, the tension around here is incredible," she said. "Everyone's goin' nuts!"

Mike chuckled. "You can't lock a hundred angry women in a small barracks and expect peace and love. Twenty of 'em have PMS, half are on the rag, and the rest are just pissed off."

"We oughtta have a party," said Yank. "Except we got nothin' to party with."

Mike thought for a minute, then snapped her fingers.

"We could get some booze if you're game. Are ya with me?"

"Whatever you say. We're all goin' to hell anyway."

Mike smiled when her taxi pulled up in front of the barracks. The Rebel flag was in the window and her favorite driver greeted her and Yank.

"How you all doin', ladies?"

The driver opened the door and Mike helped a sick-acting Yank into the car.

"This here girl is ill," she said. "We have to get her to sick bay."

The cabbie slammed the door and raced to the driver's side. Mike made sure people in the barracks were watching as the taxi sped up the hill.

"What's wrong with her, ma'am?" the driver asked.

"Marine Corps-itis," said Mike. "Take us to the NCO club."

"Oooh. I gotcha now. Hot damn, you're something else!"

When they returned to the barracks, Mike unloaded the booze near her window. Then they drove up to the main entrance and she helped Yank through the door. The woman at the duty desk had her log book ready, though she didn't seem too interested.

"What's wrong with her?" she asked.

"Some kind of poisoning," said Mike. "She'll be okay in a while."

"Do you have a chit from sick bay?"

"Oh, shit!" Mike pretended to look for the taxi. "I must have left it in the cab, on the seat. I was so busy helping her out I forgot."

"No problem," the woman said. "I'll just log you in as if you had it."

❏ ❏

A few hours later, almost everyone in the barracks had a drink in her hand. Some danced in the lounge, others talked in their rooms or roamed the halls smiling. Mike's room was the bar. Bottles lined her shelves and she made sure everyone had as much as she wanted. When supplies started running low, she went to Yank's room and closed the door.

"We may have to make another booze run," she whispered. "Maybe tomorrow."

"I dunno, Mike. Some aren't drinking. They just seem to be spyin' or something."

"Don't be so paranoid, Yank. For an Indian you sure are paranoid."

A loud knock on the door made Yank spill her drink.

"Who is it?" she asked.

Mike raced to hide the evidence.

"Duty officer. Open up."

Yank opened the door and stood at attention as Mike finished stuffing the now-empty paper cups down the back of her pants.

"What's going on in here?" the officer asked, walking into the room.

"Just visiting, ma'am."

The officer began lifting papers and checking under pillows.

"We have a report that someone brought alcohol into this barracks. I'll have to check your room."

Mike felt liquid trickling from the cups, but she didn't move. The officer looked nonchalant as she checked Yank's closet. She pulled out a small suitcase and opened it.

"What's this, Corporal?"

Looking at the bottle in the officer's hand, Yank wheezed her answer.

"Whiskey, ma'am. A present for my brother. He gets back from 'Nam next week and I have some leave coming."

"I'll have to confiscate it. It's against regulations."

The officer replaced the suitcase, then stood toe to toe with Mike.

"Let's get down to your room and see what we find, Sergeant."

Mike tenuously led the way and eyed Yank as they left. The officer was new to the barracks and didn't know the way to Mike's room, so Mike took the longest route possible.

Mike hadn't realized her room was such a mess. Bottles and cups were everywhere. The officer loaded her arms with evidence.

"These bottles are going to Civilian Intelligence, Sergeant, and you're coming with me for a blood test. I want to see just how much alcohol you have in you."

Yank passed Mike some packets of mustard as she followed the officer down the hall. While the officer was busy calling someone to give the blood test, Mike sucked the mustard and waited. She felt yellow and sour when the officer turned to face her.

"You lucked out, Sergeant. No one who gives blood tests is on duty."

Mike tried to hide her relief, but she could feel her face easing into a smile.

"We still have the bottles, Sergeant Troublemaker. You won't think you're so smart when you're sweatin' out your discharge in the brig."

❑ ❑

Wednesday, Mike reported to the company office as ordered to await the CID results. She was ready for any punishment they handed her. It would get her out of the barracks and away from the investigators and Loren. She hated Loren for using her, for taking all of her energy and what was left of her heart and mangling it into usable material for a promotion. She stood rigid while the commander read the report.

"You're off the hook, Landetti. No test, so no alcohol content in your blood. No trace of alcohol in the bottles, either. Because the bottles weren't capped, any alcohol still in them evaporated."

The commander almost smiled at Mike's triumph.

"It seems, Landetti, that the hangover I know you had was all in your head. You weren't drunk, because you weren't drinking. Score another one for the friends who took the bottle caps. The duty officer never thought about evaporation. You're dismissed."

Mike went straight to her office and pounded on her typewriter. She only used two fingers, but she could hammer out a letter almost as fast as a trained typist.

Dear Loren,
Why are you doing this? I cared about you. In some ways I still do. Turning people in for every damn little thing is not going to get you anywhere. Why don't we jam together sometime and stop all this investigation crap?
Signed,
You know who

She slipped the note under Loren's door and went into the lounge to shoot pool. Just as she was sinking the eight ball, the investigating officers tramped through the lounge on their way to Mike's office. The raging lieutenant waved Mike's note to Loren like a flag.

"We've got you now, you little pervert. Now we have proof! All we have to do is match the type in this letter to your typewriter and you're done."

Mike laughed to herself as she racked the balls for a new game. The letters would only match if they could type with two fingers. Though her office door was closed, she could hear the clacking typewriter and rising voices. Eventually, the dejected officers filed out and marched through the lounge without a glance.

"Eight ball in the corner pocket," Mike said.

PRISCILLA

Mike walked the Oceanside beach dreaming of life after the Marines. In less than four months she'd be out — free to go wherever and do whatever she wanted. The investigators had done their job. Forty-one women were leaving with general discharges. Some got pregnant; others admitted things they never did.

They didn't get Mike. She kicked at the sand with her bare feet and rolled her jeans to avoid the splashing Pacific. She didn't wear shorts anymore. The paralysis in San Diego had left her knees permanently swollen and her athletic vanity forced her to keep her legs hidden. Besides, she didn't shave her legs (as all good girls should) and people often mocked her when they noticed the dark hair.

The sand massaged her toes as she strolled by an empty beach house. When the Vacant sign caught her eye, Hollywood dreams splashed in her brain. She would live on the beach and write movies, maybe even star in a few. The data-processing courses would be finished when she mailed in the final test, and a computer job could pay the rent.

Living off base was rejuvenating. The ocean played reveille and the seagull screams were the only clue that the world wasn't perfect. Mike rushed home at the end of every day to bask in the serenity of the sunset. The weekends were saved for discreet girl watching and televised football games. Though the San Diego Chargers were now her home team, she couldn't help rooting for the Buffalo Bills.

"Once a Bills fan, always a Bills fan," she said to Yank. "Too bad you're not a sergeant yet so you could live off base. You could stay here with me and raise some hell!"

"The barracks is a drag." Yank sipped some Ripple and then emphasized a cough. "Hurts my asthma, too."

Mike patted her on the back and reached for the bottle. She massaged the bottle opening with her finger. "Seen that new sergeant? The one from Texas? Whaddaya think?"

Yank shrugged. "She's okay. If you like blondes."

"I've always had a thing for blondes," said Mike. "My first real girlfriend was a blonde. Broke my heart."

"Not me," said Yank. She smoothed her Cherokee-black hair proudly. "I only like Indians. Especially ones from Montana."

Mike flashed a teasing smile. The red-green flecks in her brown eyes shimmered in the sun.

"Only one thing wrong with Indians from Montana, Yank. They're inexperienced."

Yank looked at her and waited for the punchline as Mike readied herself to run.

"All those Indians, the ones from Montana, I mean. Every time you try to get 'em to do something they just look at ya and say, 'How? How?'"

Mike took off toward the rocks with Yank close behind. They dodged waves and scaled boulders until they reached a pier that jutted from the shore. A slow drumbeat, like the ocean's pulse, made them stop and stare at the crowds above them.

"Anti-war march," Yank said.

The Vietnam protesters carried stuffed bodies and white crosses. Mike inched closer to watch.

"We shouldn't be here, Mike. They hate military people. Bunch of 'em jumped some Marines the other night. Called them baby-killers and murderers."

"Who won?" Mike continued to gaze at the marchers as Yank climbed down to the beach.

"Nobody. They all beat the hell outta each other. Didn't change a thing. Let's go."

Mike followed her down the rocks, but couldn't help looking back at the crowd every few feet.

"Know why they all lost?" Yank asked.

They jumped to the sand and brushed themselves off.

"I asked ya if you know why they all lost?"

Mike shook her head and tried walking away from the pier, but the drumbeat seemed to suck her back.

"Weren't no Indians there," Yank said. "To tell them how!"

Mike smiled, but still the drum pounded against her senses. She thought the marchers might be right in some ways. Vietnam didn't make any sense. Killing was happening on both sides. Though she missed the friends who would never come back, she no longer wanted to kill.

"Why are we in 'Nam in the first place?"

"'Cause we're Americans, Mike. It's our job. Jesus, somebody's gotta keep the Commies from taking over the world."

"You believe that? About Commies and all? I don't."

"You'd better believe it. You're a Marine, for Christ's sake."

"Bein' a Marine doesn't make me God," Mike said.

Back at the house, Mike changed into a sweat shirt and sneakers and hid her dog tags inside her t-shirt.

"Where we goin'?"

"I don't know about you," Mike said, "but I'm gonna march."

"With them?"

"Yep."

"You can't! That's considered treason! If they catch ya they'll lock you up."

"So I won't let them catch me."

Grabbing her keys, Mike waited for Yank at the door. Yank's eyes pleaded with her.

"You're a Marine, Mike. Not one of them hippies."

"And you're an Indian. You can't believe in this war any more than I do."

"My brother fought there. He's going back for a second tour. He's lived this war, Mike, just as we have in our own way."

Yank walked out, her back to Mike.

"I'm a Marine," she said. "First, last, and always. If you go with them I can't come back here anymore."

"Do what you have to do," Mike said gently. "Just like I have to do what I'm doing. Maybe, just maybe, it'll help your brother come home alive."

As Mike watched her friend walk dejectedly away, she knew things would be different between them. The drums came closer and Mike ran up the hill to join the march. She wasn't a hippie. But she was also more than just a Marine. Too many of her friends were dead or lost. She had to help stop the war.

She marched in back of the others, testing her presence and feeling her way.

"Were you at Woodstock?"

The blonde sergeant from Texas, dressed in beads and ruffled jeans, walked beside Mike. Afraid the woman would recognize her, Mike instinctively turned her head away.

"Uh, no. No, I wasn't. But I saw the movie."

"I wasn't there either," the woman said. "I wish I was. I would have loved running naked through the fields, smokin' pot and wailin' with everyone."

Mike tried to walk a little faster, but the woman kept up with her.

"Don't worry, Sarge," she said. "I know who you are. There's Marines all up and down this beach. You're in good hands."

Mike stopped. She was caught. If one person recognized her then others might. She'd be arrested. Chanting people danced by her. She wanted to follow, but she was still a Marine. Her stomach churned and her palms sweated. The blonde took her hand.

91

"Come on, baby butch. I'll watch over you. You just keep ahold of my hand. This is the age of Aquarius, love."

As Mike let herself be led through the streets, she watched her beautiful companion cast her body in all directions. They held hands through the speeches and chants, past the uniformed Marines and sailors, back to the beach, and into the night. The woman didn't let go until she got to the rest room on the beach.

"Feel better yet?"

Mike nodded. She tried to hide her embarrassment as the woman peed, unashamedly, with the stall door open. When she finished, she went to the sink and straightened her tight sweat shirt. That was when she caught Mike staring at her in the mirror.

"As long as you're gonna look at my tits that way you might as well know my name. Priscilla. Williams. Sergeant by day, hippie all night, and lover when I find the right one to be with. You hang anywhere close to here?"

Mike choked as she tried to speak. No one had ever been so bold with her.

"I ... yeah, near here. Up ... I mean, down the beach a ways."

She tried to regain her composure as Priscilla fussed in the mirror.

"Alone? Do you hang there alone?"

Again Mike nodded.

"Do you like it that way?"

"Not always," Mike said, then managed to add playfully, "Why? Do you wanna go make mad, passionate love or something?"

Scared by her own words, she flinched when Priscilla took her hand.

"That's exactly what I had in mind, baby butch. This time, you lead."

❑ ❑

Mike's hand shook as she unlocked her door. She tried to remember if the house was clean, if the bedroom was neat.

Then she thought it wouldn't matter to a hippie. She turned on an overhead light, then quickly turned it off and chose a lava lamp instead. Priscilla breezed by the red lamp to the couch, where she pulled out a long glass pipe.

"You get the music and I'll fill the pipe."

Mike immediately obeyed, chiding herself for only having a radio. Priscilla filled the bottom of the pipe with water and loaded the bowl with marijuana.

"Blow me."

"What?" Mike thought only men used that term.

"Blow me, baby. Through the pipe. Like this."

Placing one end of the pipe in Mike's mouth, she blew smoke into Mike's lungs. Mike choked on the stinging weed.

"You're a baby at everything, aren't you, doll?" Priscilla laughed. "Now do it to me."

Mike forced as much smoke as she could into Priscilla's lungs as Priscilla swayed to the music.

"Now you," Priscilla said as she exhaled. "This time hold it as long as you can."

Mike was a little afraid of drugs, especially since the one and only time she had tried LSD. Everyone had told her acid was fun, psychedelic, erotic, peaceful. She split an Orange Sunshine with a friend and waited for her trip. At first, nothing seemed to happen. They traded jokes and stories in the barracks hallway with people who didn't know they'd dropped acid. Suddenly, they both had to go the bathroom. As if their bladders were connected to the part of the brain that reacts to drugs, they both began giggling and sweating and running and crying.

Later they separated. A "straight" friend who knew what drugs could do locked Mike in her room. A song played somewhere near the window and Mike checked her watch. The bones in her hand popped through her skin. She heard sirens and screams. The song changed and Mike couldn't stop the flowing tears. They soaked her, but she wasn't sobbing. The first song came back and so did the sirens. The screams became friends dying; the bones in her hands, bleeding rivers. She screamed to be let out, and someone finally opened the door. The people in the hall became different animals, some wild, some absurd. She slammed the door and the song changed again. After five hours, she collapsed on her bed. Her heart pounded, her clothes were soaked and she wasn't sure if anyone had really died.

She was nervous about smoking pot, but she didn't want Priscilla to have the upper hand. Priscilla's eyes danced as she blew more and more smoke through the pipe. After a few times, Mike could barely see. She heard Roberta Flack singing "The First Time Ever I Saw Your Face" and she felt her hands reaching out to the woman in front of her. She thought she danced for a while, but the same song played on and on.

The bedroom was lit in soft blue and Mike saw her body against Priscilla's. They were naked, but there was no sign of their clothes. She felt a woman's breasts caressing her face. She rolled the weight from on top of her and moved her body up and down and around and into Priscilla's. The song played on. For minutes, an hour, over and over Roberta sang. Mike felt her insides struggling against her and thought she had somehow entered Priscilla with an appendage she didn't have.

"Baby, baby," she heard. "Don't stop. Fill me up. Make me come."

The song played on as Mike pumped her body and filled the woman beneath her. Her hands were inside, then her tongue, then nothing and everything as she pumped and swayed. And still the song played on. In the morning, Priscilla was gone.

Monday, Mike hitchhiked back to base to search for her new lover. She asked everyone she met where Priscilla worked and roomed. She ran into Yank, who was cold and detached. Mike understood that Yank would have to work out her anger in whatever way she could.

Mike waited anxiously at the barracks entrance when buses and cabs brought people home after work. Finally, Priscilla arrived. Mike almost didn't recognize her. She was in full-dress uniform, her long blonde hair pinned back to regulation length and her lips painted as red as her cap cord.

Mike caught her eye as she entered, but Priscilla shot past with hardly a smile. Mike kept her distance and followed her to her room. With a glare, Priscilla closed the door in her face.

"Screw you," Mike said under her breath. She resented being a one-night stand. After hitching back to her house, she sat on the beach with a bottle of Ripple as her companion. The sunsets were earlier now, but prettier than in the summer. She thought of the colored leaves back home, the red-and-gold maples, the fall chill that thickened people's blood in preparation for winter. "Color My World" played in her head as the waves stole grains of sand from beneath her feet. She missed the changing seasons, but she loved the coastal consistency. She'd stay here and try to build a new life.

"Listen, doll. You can't be following me around base like that."

Mike jumped at the sound of Priscilla's voice.

"And especially in the barracks. I'm a sergeant by day, remember?"

Mike nodded and stared at the waves as Priscilla cuddled close to her side.

"I'm a lifer, baby," Priscilla whispered in Mike's ear as she wrapped her hands around Mike's arm. Mike naturally flexed her biceps and balanced her sitting position.

"You wanna make mad, passionate love in the sand?" Mike asked.

Priscilla squeezed her arm tighter. "As soon as you understand something. My record's clean. I keep to myself on base and do my job. You, doll, everyone knows. You don't look like any other woman, and half the bitches in the barracks have the hots for you. Not all of them know it, but it shows. You look at them with those bedroom eyes and I see them meltin' on the spot."

Reddening, Mike laughed as she lay back in the sand. "I'm not after any of those women."

"You don't have to be, baby butch. You got the charm in your walk and your talk!"

Mike tested that charm by looking deeply at Priscilla.

"Oh, yeah. That's what I mean. And you know it, don't ya?"

She spun in the sand and laid her body across Mike's lap. Mike held her and slowly kissed her.

"Now?"

"Not in the sand, baby. It gets into everything."

❑ ❑

Priscilla drove Mike to the main gate each morning, but Mike had to find her own ride from there. Priscilla didn't want anyone from the women's barracks seeing them together.

They spent weekends in bed making love to old movies on television and talking about the war. Mike wanted to take Priscilla out to dinner and dancing, but Priscilla said Mike was too obvious, "a dyke from head to toe." She was afraid of being spotted on a date with her.

"How's this?" Mike leaned in the doorway and awaited Priscilla's approval. At first, all Priscilla could do was stare. Finally, she smacked her lips.

"It works, doll. If I didn't know better, and I do, I'd swear on a country chicken that you were a dude. The moustache is the clincher. You look downright handsome!"

"Then we're goin' out," Mike said. "No more excuses. My chest is taped, my pants are stuffed, and the moustache won't come off. You're my lady and we're goin' out."

Mike reveled in her new power. If Priscilla or anyone else needed her to look like a man, she'd do it.

"The first place we're going is a shoe store," Priscilla said. "You need a pair of shit-kickers to make it perfect, and they'll make you taller. I'm buyin'."

They bought the boots and went to dinner. Priscilla said dinner would be a test to see how well Mike passed as a man. The host gave them a romantic table in the corner and smiled at them as if they were newlyweds. The waiter kept calling Mike "sir" and placed the check in front of her. After dinner they walked hand in hand to the straightest part of the beach they could find. No one gave them a second look. Mike had passed the test.

"Kiss me," Priscilla said.

Mike didn't even glance around to see if anyone was looking. She felt at one with her role and played it well. She kissed Priscilla with a stronger tenderness than ever before, smiling when she felt their bodies melt against each other.

"Tie me up, doll."

"What?" Mike laughed. "Tie you..."

"Shhh! Take me home and tie me up." Priscilla nuzzled Mike's neck.

"I want you to spread me out, tie me to the bedposts, and love me till I beg you to stop."

A familiar queasiness filled Mike's stomach and stifled the sudden panting that escaped from her chest.

"Take me home," Priscilla whispered again. "I want you. I need you to love me. Hard."

Mike tried. She tied Priscilla's hands and feet, darkened the room, and found the right music; but bondage didn't turn her on. She felt lovemaking was something that came from the heart, not external props. It wasn't a game. All she could do was laugh at the silliness of it.

When she heard the knock at the door, she quickly began untying Priscilla's wrists.

"Don't untie me. See who it is first."

After closing the bedroom door, Mike checked the front entrance. The tallest woman she had ever seen stood on the step.

"Is she here?" The woman pushed her way past Mike and surveyed the living room. Then she grabbed Mike's t-shirt and yanked her to her toes.

"I asked you if she's here?"

"Who the fuck are you?" Mike tried pushing the woman's fist away, but the stranger was too strong.

"I wanna know if the bitch is here."

"What bitch?"

The woman released her grip and dropped Mike to the floor.

"Get the hell outta here," Mike yelled.

The woman kicked open the bedroom door.

"I knew it. I knew you were here."

Priscilla's eyes bulged, and the women glared at each other in cold silence.

"You're comin' with me," the woman said.

"Hold it, asshole!" Mike tackled the woman from behind, tripping her backwards onto her back.

"I don't know who you are or what's goin' on between you two, but it sure as hell isn't going to happen here."

The woman sprang to her feet and lunged at Mike's throat. She was too big for Mike to handle. All she could feel was a giant body flattening her to the floor.

"Wait!" Priscilla screamed. "Someone untie me. Wait!"

Pinned, Mike could only watch the giant's fists pound into her. Then the taste of blood made her adrenaline surge. She rolled her body up and clenched her legs around her attacker's neck. She rolled back and forth, like a car stuck in snow, and she could hear Priscilla's screams, feel the swelling on her face, taste the blood. One final push knocked the woman off her. Mike crawled to her dresser and felt for her knife. While the stranger refocused, Mike cut Priscilla's binds, then readied herself for another attack.

"Holly! Mike! Wait!"

Priscilla stood naked between them.

"Holly?" Mike sneered. "A big son of a bitch like that and her name is Holly?"

Holly tried to grab Mike again, but Priscilla held her back.

"Would you guys please knock it off?"

"Hell, no," Mike said. "Who the hell is this Looney Tune?"

"Her lover, you jerk-off!"

Mike lowered her guard and searched Priscilla's eyes for denial. Priscilla stood speechless, obviously torn between the two. Mike closed her knife and put it in her pocket. Then she calmly tossed Priscilla's robe at her.

"Take her," she said to Holly. "And lock the door when you go."

Mike left them in the bedroom. As she walked the road to base, she quietly sang "Go Away, Little Girl."

ADOPTED
MOM

"How would you like to go home a little early, Sergeant?"

"Ma'am? I don't understand."

Mike nervously shifted her weight and stood at parade rest in front of her commander. Home was an unfamiliar word and she couldn't trust any offers made by the military. There had to be a catch, a trap. The investigations were over, Nixon was getting ready to bomb Hanoi, and Mike heard "Take Me Home, Country Roads" somewhere in the distance.

"We have a lot of openings for early Christmas discharges," the commander continued. "There are only one hundred and forty thousand men left in 'Nam and it's getting a little crowded in the ranks. You can get your honorable discharge and be home by Christmas Eve."

The thought of suddenly not being a Marine anymore, of not having a job, an identity, overwhelmed Mike. She wasn't ready. Yes, she wanted her freedom, but she wanted to control it. She felt she was being fired, stripped of an identity she was used to and still needed.

"Any chance of staying in, ma'am?"

"Let me put it this way, Sergeant. The man in charge is still out to get you. We can have you cleared through channels, honorably, before he knows what happened. If you don't go now you'll spend the next four years in jail ... or worse. I suggest you take the early out, get your conduct medal, and head on home."

Mike was rushed through the discharge process. She received her good-conduct medal while in civilian clothes. "Three years of undetected crime." The commander winked as she handed Mike her walking papers.

"We notified your parents and your local paper. They all know you're out. I'm sure there'll be someone waiting for you."

"No, ma'am. It's just me. And that's the way I like it."

Mike was escorted off base without a chance for good-byes. Home would be Oceanside and a less expensive apartment. She had neither seen nor heard from her parents in four years, and she had no intention of changing that silence.

The Godfather was the newest film in town and it forced her to think of her father, but she couldn't go back, and there seemed no reason to go back. Her parents were strangers. Somehow, she knew she loved them, and she'd never let anyone else say anything against them, but they had never really been her parents. They wanted her to be someone she wasn't, someone she could never be. Her friends were most likely living quiet, normal, and dull married lives, parenting new Fredonians who would never move away or become the people they were meant to be. She couldn't live that lie. She was different. She felt touched and protected by a God she never spoke to, and deceived and chastised by those she cared for. She'd go it alone. Maybe she'd find someone to love, and maybe she wouldn't, but she'd be happier being herself and becoming whoever she was supposed to become.

She read news stories about Calley and Attica and Germaine Greer and some guy named Chou En-Lai, and she wished she had enough money to go to the Munich Olympics. The world seemed crazy, lost in a torrent of change. It seemed lonelier, and more fragile, with no roots and shaky limbs and no direction. Mike felt her kinship.

❏ ❏

"Hello."

"Michaelene? Is that you?"

"It depends. Who's this?"

Mike heard the caller's voice choke with tears.

"It's Dad. Your father."

Instinctively, Mike pulled the receiver away from her ear. Her breath dampened the mouthpiece and her legs tightened as if poised to run.

"Michael? Michaelene?"

Her father's voice dug into her memory and sucked her back to the receiver. "I'm here."

"We heard you were out. That your enlistment's over. It was hard to find you."

Mike nodded into the phone and swallowed hard.

"We want ... Your mother and I ... Come home, Mike."

Through the stunned silence, Mike could hear her father's pain. She couldn't answer. She wanted to say no. She wanted to say yes.

"Please, Mike. We'll try again. Come home and ... Please. Come home and be my ... our daughter again."

The sob at the end of his plea was too much for Mike to endure.

"Okay," she cried back to him. "Okay."

She packed what she could carry and, using Priscilla's name as a local contact, put the rest in storage. They weren't lovers anymore, but somehow they'd managed to stay friends and often shared a beer or a ride on the roller coaster at the beach. Mike sent Priscilla a note telling her she was going home for a few weeks, but she'd be back. Then, she walked to the Pacific Coast Highway and stuck out her thumb.

"How far ya goin', Mack?"

The truck driver seemed friendly, but Mike used her toughest moves climbing into the cab.

"About three thousand miles east."

"I'm haulin' to Kentucky. Is that good enough?"

"Fine with me."

Mike stretched her legs and settled in for the long ride.

"Glad to see you're not one of those military bums," the man said. "I've seen 'em every few miles or so. Won't pick the fuckers up, though. Rather shoot 'em than ride with em', you know what I mean?"

Crossing her arms on her taped chest, Mike pretended to be sleepy.

"Shit, man! Don't go noddin' off on me. I pick up hikers for company, not to rock 'em to sleep."

"Sorry. I had a long walk today."

She tried to look interested in the scenery, but all she could see in the twilight was a dark desert and dim outlines of mountains.

"Glad it's gettin' dark," the man said. "Hit 102 degrees today. I can barrel right through now and be in Albuquerque by daybreak. Name's Manny."

Mike nodded as the truck's roar mellowed in fifth gear.

"You got a name, pal?"

"Mike."

"Mike, huh? Say, you're not one of those San Francisco fairies, are ya?"

When the driver laughed, Mike knew she had once again passed as a man.

"Picked up one the other day. Had me fooled, the damn queer. I scared his pecker off, though. Told him I chopped up fairies once in a while and made 'em talk like girls. Damn queer jumped outta the rig before I got it stopped. Left him in the desert to play with himself."

Mike feigned a laugh and a camaraderie. Manny was obviously crazy, but the desert at night was no place to talk politics or rights.

"He probably creamed his jeans and cried himself to sleep," she said.

"Ha, ha! Boy, you got that right! No one messes with Manny. Hey. I gotta take a leak. You'd better, too. It's a long haul to New Mexico."

"Don't have to," Mike said. "I've been dry all day."

Her bladder ached and her teeth shivered from the denial of nature, but Mike wasn't going to let this crazy man know she was a girl. She'd hold it as she always did when she was out in public. The last time she had walked into a public bathroom at a bus station, three women had screamed and one had batted her with a purse. She'd hold it until it was safe, even if she had to spit yellow by morning.

They sang to Glen Campbell as they passed through Phoenix, and into the night Mike listened to Manny's dirty jokes and many scores on "every woman who knows what's good." The New Mexico rest stop was dingy and dark in the dawn light, but it looked as good as morning sand to Mike.

"I'm gonna bed down outside," Manny said. "Only use the cab when it's cold. I'll catch an hour, then some chow, and we'll be on our way."

Mike watched nervously as Manny laid out his sleeping bag and loosened his pants.

"I think I'll head over there," Mike said, pointing in the general direction of the diner and rest rooms.

"Oh, sure," Manny laughed. "'Bout time you got rid of your load."

With that, he settled in and was soon fast asleep. Mike headed to the ladies' room as quickly as she could. It was early and only a few truckers were parked nearby. She stuck out her chest a little so people wouldn't think she was a man raiding the girls' room. A waitress in the diner gave her a funny look, but she didn't say anything.

A red 'Vette with New York plates pulled up to the diner just as Mike was leaving. The thought of going on with Manny made her nauseated. The 'Vette seemed a likely escape.

"Hey, Marine," she said to the man in the car, "going all the way to New York?"

The man self-consciously brushed his shaved head. "Just the state, not the city," he said.

"I just got out, too." Mike pulled her dog tags from her shirt. "I'm heading the same way. To the state."

The man looked at her anxiously.

103

"If you need a ride..."

"I do."

"Then grab what you need and hop in. I'm burning rubber after this stop. I figure two days. Tops."

Mike glanced at Manny still asleep near his truck, then followed the Marine into the diner and ordered a hot dog.

"I promised my last ride I'd buy him breakfast," she said. She ran to the truck and quietly got her sea bag. The 'Vette pulled up beside her just as she finished her note to Manny.

> Dear Asshole,
> This chopped-up wiener is for you.
> Sincerely,
> The woman Marine fairy

The 'Vette sped away as Manny sat up for his breakfast. Mike put her middle finger in the air to say good-bye.

❏ ❏

The Marine kept his promise and dropped Mike at the corner of Maple and Central avenues. When Mike looked down the hill past Hank's house and the baseball lot, she could almost see the small hedge in front of the house she'd once called home. Early buds on the maple trees tried to shake themselves loose in the wind, and Mike could smell sap oozing from the bark. She hoisted her bag to her shoulder and lingered in one last moment of indecision. An oncoming car made her shy away to avoid recognition before she was ready. This wasn't her town anymore. The scenery was the same. So was the quiet haughtiness of the people, the breeze from Lake Erie, the sidewalks that were always plowed or swept clean, even the pattern of the swaying trees. But no one here had lived what she'd lived. No one had helped her heal her scars or dry her tears. No one had shared her laughter or dreams. She'd been gone four years. In a small town, that was a lifetime. There was only one person she couldn't forget. She glanced toward Newton Street and smiled at its closeness. She was older. Things seem so tiny and insignificant when there are layers of age and experience. Still, her heart remembered. She hummed Anka's song as she sauntered down the hill.

The front door that had once locked behind her seemed larger than she remembered. She felt herself cowering, a child again, afraid to face parental judgment.

The loud doorbell tore through her fear, and she readied her defenses.

"Well, look who's here."

Her mother walked away from the open door. Hushed, angry voices came from the kitchen as Mike wrestled with her decision to enter. She could still leave. Then she heard the quick walk that signaled her father was trying to please someone. She looked up to see an old man. What was left of his hair was almost all white and lines of pain, indecision, mistakes, and sadness filled his once-robust face.

"I'll get your bag."

"I carried it this far," Mike said. "I can manage."

Her father closed the door and followed her into the hallway. Old visions crept back into Mike's soul. Her mother sat rigidly at the kitchen table, a cigarette in one hand, the other hand steadfastly at her stomach. She always held her stomach, as if the pain of womanhood and childbirth had wounded her and she needed to stop the bleeding.

"So. Put your stuff down and have some coffee. That bag isn't dirty, is it? Put it on the throw rug in case it is. Are your shoes dirty? Al, show her where the cups are, or do you remember?"

"I guess I remember."

Al nervously poured coffee for everyone. Her mother dragged on her cigarette and then took her coffee into the living room. Mike and her father sat in painful silence.

Finally, Al drew in his breath and blinked away his own fear.

"You'll have to sleep on the couch. Your mother doesn't want you in the bedroom yet."

"The couch is fine."

"She wants to make sure it's going to work out first. You know. Make sure you're going to stay."

"I guess that's up to her."

"Now, come on. It's a two-way street."

Mike put her cup in the sink.

"Looks like you did a lot of work around here," she said. "Carpets. Paneling."

"You have to wash out your cup, Mike. Your mother doesn't want you acting like a queen. She's not going to wait on you."

Mike obediently washed her cup, dried it, and put it away.

"I have to get back to work," Al said. "I'm late already."

He put on his patent leather salesman's shoes and checked his wallet.

"Where do you work now?"

"Sell liquor. Since we lost the restaurant."

He left without another word. Mike wandered into the living room to check on the couch that would be her bed. Her mother sat in the same old chair, the same old way, silently reading a dime novel. Mike couldn't stop yawning. She hadn't slept more than a few hours in three days. Her exhaustion and anxiety battled away inside her.

"Which couch is mine?"

Her mother pointed to the sofa against the far wall.

"Oh. Think I could just rest for a little while?"

"Go ahead."

"Looks like you did a lot of work around here."

"Your father did most of it. There was no one to help him."

Mike plumped a cheap pillow and stretched out on the couch.

"People say you're a queer. Is that true?"

"What? What people?"

"Everybody. I need to know. Are you queer?"

"I don't use that word."

"Well, whatever word it is, you know what I mean. Is it true?"

"Does it really make any difference?"

"You're breaking your father's heart."

"He didn't have anything to do with it."

"Then it is true."

"I don't know if it's true or not. I don't know anything right now."

"Make sure you're up in time to help with dinner."

❑ ❑

Mike and her parents went through the motions of living together as a family, and Mike avoided every confrontation her mother started. She wrote Priscilla every day, desperate to maintain some kind of contact with a life that already seemed so distant. Priscilla sent only one letter.

> Dear Mike,
> I'm living off base now and have found someone new. Some people say she looks a lot like you. I hope you don't mind, but I'm using the stuff you had in storage. We can figure it all out when and if you come back. Be good, baby b.

There was no return address.

The weather warmed quickly, and Mike was glad she still slept on the couch so she could catch the breeze through the living room windows. Her father spent most of his time on the road, and her mother maintained a cool distance whenever they were alone together. The word "queer" was only spoken one more time, by her father, who came to her in the middle of the night and cried into her chest as she held him.

"What did we do to make you like this? I'm sorry for whatever it was. I want my little girl back. Why are you like this? What did we do? Why are you a queer? Tell me what to do to help you get well."

He cried for almost an hour while Mike silently stroked his head. She didn't have answers for him. She wondered herself what made her so attracted to women. It wasn't because of some great unrequited love for her mother. It wasn't from any sexual abuse by men. Whatever the reason, it was overpowering and all-consuming. It wasn't something to be explained or defined. It was like love itself, defiant in its strength and mystifying in its power. She wondered if her father could explain why he loved women any better than she could. Or if her mother had an answer for why she had married a man when she obviously wasn't happy with the consequences.

"I'm going to the fairgrounds to look for work."

"Why the fair?" her father asked. "What about looking into college? The coach says he'd like you at Fredonia State. To train you for the Olympics."

"I can't be in the Olympics, Dad."

"You could if you tried. Everyone always talked about the way you could run."

"I was paralyzed in the Marines. I'll never be a runner again."

She saw tears welling in her father's eyes and quickly closed the door behind her so she wouldn't see him cry.

She stood among a half dozen other hopefuls waiting for the extraordinarily beautiful woman in the office to hand out assignments. Mike couldn't take her eyes off her. Her background showed in every gesture, every perfect seam and line. When the woman smiled, Mike felt like a knight ready to serve her every whim.

"I'm sorry, young man. There are no more jobs."

Mike looked behind her to see who the woman was talking to.

"I'm talking to you. We're fresh out of jobs."

"Oh. I'm not a man."

The woman looked startled and then embarrassed, but Mike didn't want her to be.

"Don't worry," Mike said. "Everyone makes the same mistake. It's the short hair or something. I can do anything you ask me to. Guard the gate. Paint. Work in the office. I can do anything."

The woman looked at her softly. "Can you make it sunny and warm for the entire week?"

"If I put my mind to it."

"Then we can use you. I'm Betty Dellman. Most people call me Betty D. because there's so many Bettys around here."

She shook Mike's hand graciously and Mike could hardly let go.

"I read palms, too," Mike said.

"Really." Betty turned her hand over to let Mike look at her palm. "What do you see in mine?"

Mike studied the lines carefully, wincing at what she saw and felt.

"Your heart line is broken; someone has hurt you very much."

Betty looked at the others in the office who were mesmerized by the reading. She smiled at Mike, but Mike could tell the palm wasn't lying.

"You're very smart and very in control, and you had an illness. You still have it. But you're fighting it."

"What kind of illness?" Betty asked seriously. The others in the office seemed shocked.

"Cancer, I think. Or something like it."

Betty took back her hand and laughed. Mike felt her hiding her pain.

"That's a good act, kid. Where'd you learn to do that?"

"I used to go fishing at Lily Dale. You know, that spiritualist place on Casadaga Lake? They told me I have the mystic *M*."

"Hmmm. Maybe you *can* make it sunny all week. Can you read my mind and tell me what job you'll have first?"

"Painting chairs. Green."

"You're smart, kid. You saw the chairs piled near the hall, right?"

Mike nodded and smiled impishly.

"There are over three hundred of them and they have to be painted by next week. By hand. How many do you think you can finish?"

"As many as you want me to."

❏ ❏

Within a few days, Betty and Mike acted like old friends. Betty picked her up on the corner and drove her to work. As Mike painted chairs, she sang "Alone Again" and Garland and Sinatra, and was constantly surprised by Betty's thoughtfulness. Betty made sure she was warm and fed and not too lonely. She called the hall to make sure Mike took breaks and came back to the office for coffee. Betty was twenty-five years older than Mike, but together they looked and acted like teenagers.

Each night after work, they went to the Inn across from Betty's house and told jokes, laughed, listened to music, and waited for Betty's husband to show up so they could drink some more before dinner.

Betty's favorite song was "Softly." Often, when they drank longer than they should have, Mike would put a dozen quarters in the jukebox and sing the song over and over to a delighted Betty.

When the fair was over, they had a farewell party at the Inn. Mike's heart sank at the thought of not being with Betty anymore.

"I have something to tell you," she said to Betty while they toasted margaritas. "You might hate me for it, but I have to tell you."

"Go ahead and tell, kid. I'm listening."

"I think I'm gay."

"So. Did you expect me to be shocked?"

"I guess so. It's not something you hear every day."

"Well, I'm not shocked. Now what do you want to talk about?"

"'Softly. I will leave you, softly. For my heart would break, if you should wake, and see me go.'"

"Oh, good job, kid. Thanks a lot. Now you're trying to get me all mushy. I'll be here every day at five and a margarita will be waiting for you. I'm not going anywhere."

They met every day, joined friends at parties, played cards, and stayed up all night talking and listening to music. Mike felt like a kid and a husband. She took care of Betty when she had too much to drink, forced herself to stay awake if Betty needed the company, and defended her if friends got drunk and pushy. She made Betty her life, and Maple Avenue got nasty again.

"Nothing's changed with you," her mother said. "You still put everyone else first. Your friends are still more important than family. You, you idiot. How do you think it makes us feel? Makes us look to the jerks around here?"

"Maybe if you didn't worry so much about what everyone else thinks, you could act like a human being once in a while."

"Why, you ungrateful brat!" Her mother swung to slap her across the face, but Mike caught her arm.

"You wanted to make me tough and now I am. I wouldn't swing if I were you."

"I'm your mother! I don't expect you to like me, or even to love me—"

"Don't worry, I don't."

"—But I do expect you to respect me. I'll beat you within an inch of your life if I have to."

Mike dropped her mother's hand and stuck out her chin.

"Go ahead. Hit all you want. I won't cry. I won't turn away. Have your fun."

Her mother raised her hand again but stopped her swing just in time. Mike saw the hatred in her eyes, felt the poison in her heart, and couldn't hold back her own tears. She clenched her face and shook as she quickly brushed away the streaming salt water from her cheeks.

"You can't hurt me anymore, Mom. Nothing you do can hurt me anymore."

She was turning to leave when her father walked in the door. He was a quick defender of his wife, no matter what the circumstance, and Mike still feared his rage. She shrugged to show him the incident was out of her control, but she knew he couldn't see. He was blinded by his need to protect his wife.

"I'll pick up my things tomorrow and be on my way."

"They'll be on the porch, young lady," her mother said. "I don't want another scene like today."

Mike went straight to the Inn to wait for Betty. She'd have to leave, maybe go back to California where she really wanted to be anyway. She wanted to make it easy on Betty. They drank and joked and talked until early morning. All the while, Mike knew Betty was waiting to be told. Arm in arm, they shuffled through the leaves to Betty's house.

"Things change too quickly," Mike said.

"Nothing has to change, kid. The seasons are reality. Change is reality. But reality doesn't have to change, and it doesn't have to be bad if you don't want it to."

"I got thrown out again, Betty."

"Then you'll live here, with me and Bob. And you'll figure out what you're going to do with your life and get on with it. You can't keep running back and forth every time the weather changes."

"But I'm not easy to live with. I get crazy or something. Like a trapped animal."

"I'm not easy either, kid. And believe me, neither is Bob. You'll be helping me by staying here."

Of course there was nothing Mike wanted more than the opportunity to be with Betty as much as possible, but living in her house made her feel like a child, like Betty and Bob were the parents, and they seemed to relish it. They took her everywhere with them and people started referring to her as their kid.

"You were right when you read my palm," Betty said. "I had cancer. I'm almost cured. It'll be seven years pretty soon. But it meant I could never have kids. You play your cards right and life could be pretty good for you."

"I don't want your money. I love you, for God's sake. Money doesn't love or care."

Betty looked at her with the smile Mike loved. "So you finally said it. I've been waiting and waiting. You finally said it."

"So what?" Mike was embarrassed. "You knew it already. What difference does it make?"

"Don't get your back up, kid. You needed to say it so you wouldn't feel so bad about it."

"Yeah? Well, what about you? You love me too, you know."

"You're right. But I didn't have to say it to make myself feel better."

Betty opened her arms and Mike hugged her close. She wanted her like she had never wanted anyone before, but she knew she could never have her. They'd love as well as they could, but Betty would always be coming from a different place, from a life she was afraid to leave. She didn't love Bob, but she was married to him. To her, it was a contract and a debt that she could never back out of. Bob cheated on Betty with his secretary, frequently came home drunk, and often tried to rape his wife before deciding to hit her instead. Mike caught him only once. She put her body between his and Betty's and dared Bob to go through her. She expected him to hit her. Instead, he took off his pants and asked her if she'd ever been laid.

"That's all you need, you know. Just get laid. It'll straighten you right out. You'd like to sleep with my wife, wouldn't ya? Wouldn't ya? I know. I see you two together. The Bobbsey twins. Well I got news for ya, butch. She don't sleep with anyone. Not me. Not you. Not anyone. Get laid, kid."

His shorts bulged as he swayed drunkenly, daring her to take him on. Mike almost felt sorry for him. He had never treated her badly. He was a screwed-up man who thought his wife should always serve him. His poor male ego was threatened by Betty's abstinence.

"Sleep it off, Bob," Mike said. "You don't want this any more than I do."

She put an arm around his shoulder and led him to the stairs.

"We'll watch football together tomorrow, just you and me. Go sleep it off."

Sure that he was safely upstairs, Mike went to Betty and held her limp body in her arms.

"You're nice to him because of me," Betty said.

"He's your husband. As long as you want him, and I see that's what you want, I'll be nice to him. If I hurt him it would hurt you. And I won't do that."

❏ ❏

Deciding to make the most of a new trend, Mike enrolled in a ten-week computer-programming course in nearby Buffalo. Betty acted the parent role so Mike could secure financial aid, then helped her move into a motel.

"I'll send you care packages every week, and I expect you home on weekends."

Betty trembled when they said their good-byes, and Mike tried to reassure her. "I'm only fifty miles away. Bob won't hurt you knowing I'm this close. I'll take the first bus out every Friday."

Mike kept her promise. For ten weeks, she took the bus back to Betty and stayed up the whole weekend to be with her. She still was at the top of her class when she finished and took the last bus home.

"Mike? Is that you?"

She stepped off the bus and looked up into Sharon's eyes.

"Hi. I, uh ... just got in from Buffalo." Mike almost had to stand on her toes to meet Sharon's eyes. "Still in Fredonia, huh? I thought you'd be married and gone by now."

"You're not married, are ya, Mike?"

"Oh, God, no. Are you?"

"Not yet."

Each waited tensely for the other's words. Mike couldn't find any. She had never thought she'd see Sharon again. The strange thing was that Sharon acted like she didn't remember what had happened between them, like they were passing friends with no history and, obviously, no future.

Sharon finally broke the silence. "It was nice to see you, Mike."

Mike could only nod. She watched Sharon walk all the way down the street, hoping she would give some sign that she remembered how much Mike had loved her. But Sharon was in her own world. Mike kicked herself for not being more charming or talkative. Sharon seemed to be doing well. Mike decided she shouldn't think about her anymore. Besides, she had work to do. Betty was going to help her send out resumes and drive her to interviews. She had her own life to worry about.

EIGHT CATS, TWO DOGS

Almost immediately, Mike got a job interview with a firm in Texas. They liked her military background and the fact that she was number one in her class. The interview process was long and complicated, but they finally offered her a job.

"Texas isn't so far away, Betty. It's good money. And I'll be able to come home a lot."

Betty sat in her usual place on the porch, rocking back and forth with her arms crossed in front of her. Mike knew how much she hurt, but this was her chance to have a career with an important company that was willing to pay her well for her talent. She didn't really want to leave, but she also didn't want to spend the rest of her life weighing grapes or waiting on tables.

"Betty, can't you understand? You knew I'd have to find a job somewhere. You even helped me."

"Ha. That's just what I wanted to hear, kid."

"Oh, you know what I mean. We have to cut the umbilical cord."

"Is that what you think?"

"Well, isn't that what's going on?"

Bob came onto the porch all smiles and gin.

"Hey, kid, I'm proud of ya. That's a damn good company you hooked up with. Come on inside. I wanna talk to you for a minute."

Betty waved her hand, letting Mike know it was okay to leave her. Bob pulled two chairs close together so he could talk quietly.

"Look, kid. You and I have had our ups and downs, but basically we're friends, right? I mean, you live here and we both kind of take care of Betty, more or less. Well, what I'm gonna tell ya is either gonna make ya mad, or happy as hell."

He got a cockeyed smile on his face and took another drink.

"I got a chance to go all the way," he said. "I mean the divorce bit, a new wife and a little happiness. I don't know when exactly, we gotta work some things out, you know? But the thing is, Betty's gonna need someone around. I'm going to send you a check once you get to Texas. A big check. I want you to have a good time. Then I want you to invite Betty down and show her a good time. You two are naturals at partying. Once she's down there, I'll call up and break the news. I don't want you hurting her, now. I'm counting on you to take care of her."

Bob patted her knee and smiled with one eye closed. Mike shoved his hand away and grabbed his drink from his hand.

"You're drunk. And out of your fucking mind."

"Now, Mike. I might be a little drunk, but I know what I'm sayin'."

"Well, count me out, mister. I'm not going to be part of your little game."

"Okay, okay. I shocked you a little. Just stay calm. It's gonna happen sooner or later. I just thought you might want to help her out a little. I don't want ya to ever hurt her."

"What about you? Aren't you hurting her?"

116

"Nah! She's got friends, like you. She'll be fine."

Mike spent the next two days walking through the cemetery and up and down the hills. She wouldn't play Bob's game, but she was afraid of what Bob would do once she was gone. No matter what she did or said, Bob would probably follow through with his plan. Mike couldn't decide whether or not she should warn Betty. She'd suffered from being the messenger once before. When she had told a wife about her husband's advances, the wife had blamed her for everything. She didn't want to risk losing Betty because of Bob's stupidity.

"I turned down the Texas job. I want you to help me look for another."

"You're not going?"

Mike shook her head and Betty hugged her tightly.

"But why, kid? That was the perfect job."

"They wanted me to pay my way there and live in an expensive hotel near the office. Things like that. It just didn't sound like such a good deal to me."

Privately, Mike asked forgiveness for her lie. The company had offered to pay for everything, especially after she'd turned them down. She didn't want Betty to even suspect that she had rejected the job for her. She'd find a position closer to Fredonia and try not to change the things they were now so used to. She'd spend her weekends with Betty and come home some nights to check on her. She owed it to her. She loved her.

❑ ❑

Within a few weeks, Mike got a call from a better company. IBM liked the way she had tested and wanted her for a second interview. Betty drove her into Buffalo and waited at a nearby restaurant.

The personnel manager put a fatherly arm around Mike's shoulder and guided her into his office.

"We want to make you a customer engineer," he said. "You did well in electronics. You'd be our first woman ever to fix mainframe computers."

117

"I thought I was testing to be a programmer," Mike said.

"Oh, you were. But I saw the electronics background and knew you'd be happier this way. It pays more money than programming and it's right up your alley. It has an easier career path, too. You could be a field manager in just a few years."

Mike told Betty she was accepting the offer, then packed her things and left for twelve weeks in Manhattan. IBM's training center was in Rockefeller Center, and all potential engineers were paid twenty-four dollars a day — twelve dollars to split the cost of a hotel room, and twelve for food.

Betty quickly made Mike some pantsuits that seemed a little too feminine and Bob said his usual good-bye, which consisted of reminding Mike to get laid. She arrived in New York excited and ready to start work. She was already on salary and could save that money while she lived off the company in the Big Apple.

After picking up her room key, Mike headed to the seventh floor of the Statler. She was about to walk in when she remembered she might have a roommate. She decided to knock. When the door opened, a man in boxer shorts greeted her with delight.

"IBM?"

Mike nodded.

"Great! We're roommates! Come on in!"

"You're my roommate?"

"Yep! For twelve weeks. They never had a girl in this class before. Everyone was bettin' you'd chicken out. Wait'll I tell the guys I won!"

"You won?"

"Yep. We had bets on who'd get the girl."

"Sorry, Charlie, or Bill, or Dick, or whoever you are. We're not roommates. I'll get my own room if you don't mind."

"But the company won't pay for it! If you get a single, you'll have to foot the bill. And so will I!"

"Well, if I were you, I'd tell the guys to pay up and help you cover the cost of the room."

118

Mike breezed through the training. Most of the people in her class didn't have her strong electronics or data-processing background, so the courses were taught simply. The hands-on training was a little different. The guys in her class roomed and studied together and helped one another figure out mechanics. None of them welcomed the chance to help the girl who beat them on their tests.

She wrote Betty every day, and the ten weeks went by quickly. Betty never wrote back, but Mike understood that she was probably too busy drinking and dealing with her life.

When she returned to Buffalo, the first thing she had to do was find a place to live. She went back to the motel she had stayed in during programming school and called old classmates to ask if they knew a good place to start. Some of them were locals and Mike wanted their input before she ended up on the wrong side of town.

Diane, who had been third in the class, had a programming job with a bank and was more than willing to help. Mike let her drive her around town to look at apartments, and she welcomed the companionship.

"The first thing I'm gonna do is buy a car," Mike said. "And I'll never pass a hitchhiker or let anyone drive me anywhere again."

"With the kind of money you're making you'll have a car in no time."

"A sports car. I'm gonna get a sports car. And a stereo that's all mine. And someday I'll buy a house, maybe two."

Diane laughed. "That's some dream you've got there."

"I'll get trained in every machine IBM has, so I'm indispensable. They said I could make manager in a few years. Then maybe I can ask for a transfer. To San Diego."

"Tell you what, Mike. I need a place to live, too. To get away from my parents. Why don't we find a two-bedroom apartment and share the expenses? That way you can save half your money."

"I'm not sure. I mean, I'm sure it would be okay. But I'm hard to live with. I've got this thing about freedom."

"You don't have to answer to me. Just come home in time to pay your half of the bills."

Mike thought about the car she wanted and the money she'd never had. By sharing an apartment, she could save money for college, get some kind of filmmaking degree, and go to Hollywood. Everything was going her way.

They found an apartment, really half a house, and Mike immediately bought furniture.

"I can't help you pay for this, Mike. I don't have the same kind of job you have."

"Don't worry about it. Someday you'll have your own place and your own furniture. You're just using mine while you're here."

As soon as Mike had saved enough money, she bought a Triumph Spitfire convertible and showed it off to her boss. She liked Chuck. He wasn't much older than she was, and she knew he got harassed a lot for being the only field manager with a female in his group. She handled her accounts and went to one new school after another. The problem with being so well trained was that Mike got called out at any hour of the day or night to fix a machine that was vital to someone's business. Often, she'd be scheduled for a machine upgrade that had to be done after midnight, the only time most businesses could afford to shut down. Too often, she had to do the upgrades alone. Other engineers' wives didn't want their husbands locked in a warehouse or computer room with another female.

But Mike prided herself on never missing a workday. She bought the things she wanted, spent money on Betty and other friends, and enjoyed her freedom. Each month, she went to the SPCA and picked out a cat or a dog to bring home. Diane loved animals and helped to train them, so they weren't very much bother. Each morning, Mike would let them all out while she took a shower. After her morning coffee, she'd go out on the porch and whistle. The cats lined up in chronological order while the golden retriever watched over them. Sometimes, she'd have to call them in by name. She lived in an Italian neighborhood, and whenever the neighbors heard her calling they'd come outside to watch the parade.

"Ally, Annie, Casey, Cisco, Dallas, Billi, Acki, Abu."

Mike became known as the Cat Woman of Bird Avenue.

"I lost my job today," Diane said. "They fired me for missing so much time."

"When did you miss the time? I thought you went to work every day."

"Well, some days I stayed home. I just didn't like it there. I don't know what I'm going to do now."

"Just find another job."

"That's easy for you to say. You never have any trouble doing anything."

Diane looked at her sheepishly. Mike could smell trouble.

"I don't want to leave here, Mike. I want to keep living with you."

"That's fine. I'll cover for you till you find another job."

"I don't want to find another job. I wanna be ... well, kinda your wife."

"My what? Are you kidding? What makes you think I would want a wife?"

"You do."

"No, I don't."

"Yes, you do. Everybody does. And, besides, we've lived together long enough for you to tell the truth."

"The truth about what? What is this?"

"Who's Betty?"

"None of your business."

"Is she your girlfriend?"

"She's twice my age, for Christ's sake."

"Aha! I was right. If you were straight you would have just said no."

"What do you mean, if I was straight?"

"You're not. You sleep with women."

"I don't sleep with anybody."

"But you'd like to sleep with women. You're in love with this Betty, aren't you?"

"I care about her. She's very special to me. She's kind of an adopted mother."

"But you're in love with her, aren't you?"

"I told you. Yes, of course I love her."

"You don't just love her. You're *in* love with her. You're a dyke, aren't you?"

"I don't even know what a dyke is."

"A lesbian. A woman who loves women. A woman who doesn't love men."

Mike thought about all the feelings she had for Betty and the leftover heartbreak for Sharon and Sue and Priscilla. No one had ever defined her before. They had called her names and accused her of things, but no one had ever labeled her. She loved because it came naturally. It had never occurred to her that there was an analysis of her loving.

She turned away from Diane to hide the tears that were choking her. She felt thirteen or fifteen or whatever age it is that people realize who they are. Diane came up to her back and hugged her from behind.

"It's okay. I'm kind of a dyke, too. I've slept with women. Maybe we can help each other."

They decided to sign up for a class together at the university titled "Women in Crisis." It was part of a new women's studies program and they were sure that, sooner or later, someone would bring up dykes or lesbians. They sat on opposite sides of the class so that no one would know they were together and listened to personal histories of women who had been raped or molested or beaten. At home, they pretended to be married. The cats and dogs were their children, and Mike worked to provide.

So that she could work on her degree, Mike signed up for more night classes. Between overtime at IBM and credit hours in college, she was gone almost ninety hours a week.

Mike tried to write Betty often and made sure Diane wasn't home whenever Betty came to visit.

"You're going to have to change, Mike," Betty said over a weekend dinner. "I know what's going on in Buffalo. I've always accepted who you are, as long as you weren't practicing it. And don't get me wrong, I won't stop you from being who you are. But if you ever decide that you're going to stay gay, that you're not going to change and you're sure about it, I want you to tell me."

"And then what? We're not friends anymore? Or family? Or whatever the hell we are?"

"Then it's up to me. If I can accept it, I will. But if I can't, well, then that's that."

"Betty, do you hear what you're saying? You're saying that if I'm ever convinced I'm going to keep feeling love for women, the same love I've felt for you for two years, that's when you'll stop loving me."

"Are you telling me that's how it is now?"

"I don't know how it is now. Right now, I don't think I want to love anybody, and I don't know who I love. Including you."

She tried to turn her back to walk away, but Betty's pull was too strong.

"No, no. That's not true. I do love you. And I don't ever want to hurt you. I'll try."

"You'll try what?"

"To be normal, or whatever. I don't know. I'll just try to be what you want me to be."

Mike signed up for English courses and got carried away with Mark Twain. She loved school. It was exciting and different and something she needed. Her favorite English teacher was divorced, with a learning-disabled son named John. Mike often went to Janet's house to talk about Twain and visit with John. She'd return home late, fight with Diane about her freedom, and then get called out to service a machine. She finally asked for reassignment to the parts department to recover from her exhaustion. Diane told her it was a mistake. She had ordered new rugs and they needed the overtime. Mike didn't care. Her body was tired. She worked normal hours, went to school, visited John, and came home to sleep.

"Mike? This is your neighbor. Zo. You'd better get home right away. Your roommate is killing the cats!"

Mike raced home in her convertible. Seeing all her doors and windows open, she thought at first that she'd been robbed. Zo waited on the porch next door.

"They're gone, Mike. I have one of your cats up here. I think his leg is hurt. I don't know what she did with the rest. The whole neighborhood is looking for them."

Mike could only look at her and nod. She slowly climbed the stairs to her apartment, quietly listening for a cat or dog, and silently praying that everything was okay. Her apartment was empty. Every record and book, every piece of furniture, even the dishes Betty had given her were gone. A note on the counter sent her into a rage.

"Dear Mike," it said, "I deserve these things more than you because you're working and I'm not. I know you're screwing that teacher. Don't try to find me."

Mike stumbled down the stairs to her car and raced to Diane's parents' house. Diane's father met her at the door.

"Come any closer and we call the cops," he said.

"You won't have to call the cops. I'm calling 'em. Your daughter stole everything I own."

"She only took what was rightfully hers."

"Where is she? I'll show her what's hers!"

"My daughter is underage and you're a queer. Oh, yes, she told us all about it. All the disgusting details. The threats you made on her life, just as you are now. She told us all of it. I don't condone my daughter's actions, selling her body to you the way she did. But as long as she sold it, you're paying."

"You people are fucking crazy! I'm going to the cops, mister, and your daughter's going to jail!"

"They lock up queers who seduce and molest minors. I suggest you think twice before you turn yourself in."

JOHN'S
RAINBOW

Mike drove through the Buffalo streets half the night searching for her cats and two dogs. Near dawn, she sat by the waterfront debating her next move. Diane's father was probably right. He was a big shot in the school system, and his power would negate Mike's story. If she went to the cops, they would only see a queer. She'd end up at the short end of the stick. It was just money. Losing the records bothered her the most: many of them had been gifts commemorating special times. The rest of the stuff carried no special meaning. Except for the animals. They were gone, alone or dead, lost forever in a world that wouldn't care. She could forgive someone wanting money or material comfort; she could even understand lying to survive, but she would never forget and could never forgive destroying life.

She thought about going to Betty for comfort, but Betty would have to know the whole story and Mike had purpose-fully kept some of her life confidential. Betty wouldn't under-stand. It would only be another mark, a score, to move Mike further away from women. Mike didn't want that. She didn't think other people's actions should determine her identity.

She drove to Janet's and waited for morning. John would need a ride to his special school and Janet would at least listen to what had happened with a kind of detached awareness.

"Can I ride in the front with you? Like a big person does? Can I, Mike?"

"Sure. You wanna drive, too?"

"Noooo. You're just teasing."

John's smile immediately warmed Mike. She felt her anger float away. John was a special little friend. As far as Mike was concerned, his six years of life had given him more insight, compassion, and love than most adults would ever know.

"Will you sing to me today?"

"Whatever you want, Johnny. You name it."

"That one you sang some yesterdays ago. That one about birds flying over the rainbow."

"That's your favorite?"

Johnny nodded with a sad smile, and Mike touched his knee to comfort him.

"Rainbows are nice," Mike said.

"Yeah. 'Specially if you're a bird, a kid-bird, and you can fly over them when grown-ups make bad storms."

Mike sang John's song as softly as traffic would allow and drove slowly so she'd have time to finish it. As she pulled the car to the curb she got an unexpected, very tight hug from the little boy next to her.

"I love you," he said. "I wish you were my grown-up."

Though John was capable of walking into school alone, his special-education teacher came out to escort him and seemed to shield John from Mike's wave.

Afterward, Mike told Janet what had happened with Diane and was immediately invited to move in with her and John.

Mike had nothing to move but her clothes and a suitcase full of small memories, so she was all moved in when John came home from school that day.

"You mean you'll be in the room right next to mine? Every morning? And you can take me to school?"

Nodding at his every question, Mike delighted in the joy on John's face. His little hand gently squeezed hers.

Every morning, John woke up and called to Mike from his bedroom. And every morning, Mike growled and told him to get out of bed. The growl always sent John into joyous giggles. Soon, he started calling Mike "Bear" and reveling in the special name.

Once, out of loneliness or need or plain curiosity, Mike and Janet tried sleeping together. But the attraction wasn't there, and they spent the night on opposite sides of the same bed. John was surprised when Mike's growl and Janet's prodding came from the same room.

"Here, Mommy, you can have Teddy from now on."

After John handed Janet his favorite stuffed animal, she wiped the tears from his eyes.

"What's wrong, Johnny? Did Teddy do something to hurt you?"

John shook his head and looked at Mike.

"Then what's wrong?" Janet asked. "Why are you giving me Teddy?"

"I don't want you to steal my Bear," he said. "You take Teddy and I'll keep Mike."

"That kid has the most fragile heart I've ever seen," Mike later said to Janet.

"It's just his learning disability. A lot of kids with his problem are like that. They're oversensitive and sometimes a little weird."

"I don't think that's weird at all. If learning disabilities make people as loving as he is, the whole world should get disabled."

Mike played Santa for John, making sure he had every present he had ever asked for. The model train was John's favorite, and Mike spent countless hours pretending to go on train trips with John as the engineer.

"His disabilities are getting worse," Janet said. "The doctors want to put him on a new drug to stop the short circuits between the two sides of his brain."

Mike made phone calls and borrowed dozens of books from the library so she could learn all there was to know about learning disabilities. One fact that stood out as most closely related to John was the possibility of allergies as a cause for symptoms. Mike noticed that every time John went to his father's house for the mandatory weekend stay, he came home more disconcerted and tense and he seemed to lose his sense of time and space. Mike wanted to know everything she could about John's father: his habits, his house, even his clothes. But her questioning of Janet seemed to give rise to old scars that caused loud arguments between her and Mike. Once, overhearing one of the arguments, John carefully and silently took Mike's hand and led her outside. He pulled Mike down next to him on the step. With adultlike gestures, he leaned forward and clasped his hands together to talk to Mike.

"You have to understand my mommy, Mike. Her heart is different than our hearts. Sometimes her heart bleeds so hard that it makes her face very red. And sometimes it bleeds so hard it makes her voice louder. Don't be mad at her, Bear. She's just a mommy with a broken heart."

Mike listened in awe. From then on, she made absolutely sure she and Janet never fought when he might be listening.

Two weeks before John was scheduled to go to his father's for the summer, he came home from school as disturbed as he'd ever been after a weekend away. Suspecting a connection, Mike raced back to John's school to find the answer. The teacher seemed upset by Mike's presence, but she answered all Mike's questions about John's day. Mike found what she was looking for.

"It's the clay, Janet. John's father does pottery, right? He works with clay in the house, right? John worked with clay today at school. There's clay dust all over the place. He's allergic to it. Maybe other things too, but definitely clay. That's what triggers this so-called short-circuiting!"

"What am I supposed to do about it? I can't tell his father to stop working with clay."

"Tell him about the allergy. Tell him to keep John away from the room where he works. Tell him anything. For John's sake."

"I'll try. He doesn't listen very well. I'll try to tell him when he comes to pick John up for the summer."

That night, Mike and John sat together on the couch to watch *The Wizard of Oz*. Mike had promised special television time so that John could hear Garland sing.

"I wish I could go over the rainbow someday."

"You can, Johnny. Just believe that you can and you'll fly like a bird anytime you want."

"Are people smart over there?"

Mike hugged John close to her. "No smarter than you are, buddy. Not even half as smart."

They watched until Dorothy started down the yellow brick road. Mike felt John's body shaking next to her and his face was streaked with tears.

"Johnny? What's wrong, honey?"

John's body shook violently and his eyes were closed tightly as he cried. Mike wrapped him in her arms and kept her cheek next to his.

"Go ahead, Johnny. Shake it out. Let it all out, honey."

"Am I bleeding, Bear? Is there blood on my face?"

"No, sweetheart. Those are tears, honey. Just tears. Go ahead and let them out."

"Am I dying, Bear? Am I bleeding?"

"Just tears, honey. They need to get out. Shake them out. Cry, sweetheart. Bear's right here with you. Go ahead and cry. Cry it out."

"Don't leave me, Bear. Don't leave me. Don't leave me."

John finally slowed his shaking, and Mike carried him to his bedroom. John wouldn't let go, so Mike kept him against her and lay on her back so that John stayed close against her chest. Each time she'd try to move away, he'd grab hold and awaken. She stayed with him through the night. By morning, she was able to roll him off. He awoke with a smile.

"Are you okay, buddy?"

"Sure, Bear. What are you doing in here?"

Mike convinced Janet that the allergies were serious. She explained that John's incident was just like many LSD trips she had seen in the Marines, and that if the allergies didn't make him crazy, the drugs could kill him.

"If you can't convince his father to do something, I will," Mike said. "If he loves this kid he'll do it."

When John's father came for him, Mike listened from the kitchen to make sure Janet convinced him that something needed to be done about the allergies. But Janet was afraid of her ex-husband and backed down when he questioned her. Mike had no choice but to interfere.

"Hi. I was just having lunch and I heard something about food allergies or something. I've done a lot of work on this kind of stuff if you need any help."

"Bear knows all kinds of things, Dad. Don't you, Bear?"

"Bear?"

John's father looked at Mike, then at John.

"This is Bear? The one you're always talking about?"

"Yep. That's my Bear."

"I thought Bear was ... John led me to believe ... Never mind. Let's go."

He pulled John away from Janet and Mike waved good-bye.

"I'll be back soon, Bear. Don't go away."

"I'll be right here."

Digging her hand into Mike's shoulder, Janet spun her around.

"Are you crazy? Do you want me to lose my son?"

"What are you talking about? I just wanted to help..."

"Help who? John's father is a paranoid homophobe. Now he knows about you now. He's seen you."

"So what the hell can he do about it?"

"He can take John away from me, that's what he can do."

"Oh, come on. Are you telling me a court would take your son away from you just because I'm in your house?"

"You're damn right that's what I'm telling you. I've told you a million times to keep out of sight when that man is around. Why couldn't you stay in the kitchen?"

"Because you were too much of a chicken-ass to tell him what he needed to be told."

"And he still doesn't know, does he?"

"No. But that's not my fault. You know, all you so-called feminists are exactly alike. You run around tootin' your horns about being aggressive and assertive with your bullshit definitions and radical analysis, but when it comes to real life, the stuff that makes dreams and decisions and childhood and life, all the things that make life worth it, you back down and run away. You blame everything on someone else. If you gave a shit about John you never would have let him go back there until the clay crap was taken care of. You never would have let him out the door."

"I care about him. He's my son. He's not yours, he's mine."

"That's right, he's yours. But he's a boy. And boys grow up to be men, right? And all the crap you're reading and all the baggage you're carrying around tells you men are the enemy. Well, your son is not your enemy. He's a boy. But he's also a kid. A kid with a heart that doesn't know or care about what gender it is, and neither should you. And your ex-husband? A paranoid homophobe? Then make him paranoid! Show him your power and give him some reality to be afraid of. John needs you to do that."

"John will survive. He's been okay this long."

"John is sick, Janet."

"Well, he makes me sick, too. Do you think it's easy raising a kid who's learning disabled? He'll never be smart. Never be able to really take care of himself. It's not easy. It's hard. Hard on me! And I count, too. I have needs, too. I have a life to live. It's hard."

Mike put a hand on Janet's shoulder to soothe her sobs.

"Who do you think has it the hardest, Janet? You? Or your son?"

❑ ❑

Mike spent the summer taking women's studies courses and putting in extra hours at IBM. She got placed with a new

131

field manager, an ex-Marine who believed all women should stay in the kitchen or the bedroom. He hated working with a woman engineer. In an attempt to force Mike to quit, he increased her workload to nearly ninety hours a week. Though she made money in overtime, the pressure finally overcame her. For the first time in three years, she called in sick. She couldn't move, and could barely speak. Her body collapsed in total exhaustion. Though offered unlimited sick days, Mike's manager ordered her to report to work or bring in a written doctor's excuse.

"You've never asked any of the guys for something in writing," she said.

"From you we want something in black and white."

"I'll give you something in black and white. Tomorrow at eight."

She pulled herself from bed the following morning and used a black pen to write her resignation. Unemployment didn't scare her. She had saved enough money to finish another semester of college. She would just add extra credit hours to her schedule and finish her degree in record time.

After recovering from her exhaustion, Mike spent two weeks helping IBM's top management write women engineers into the employee handbook. Then, she painted John's room so it would be ready when he returned from his father's.

Janet waited in the doorway as Mike put the finishing touches on a rainbow across John's wall.

"What do ya think?"

"He won't be back."

"Who won't be back? What are you talking about?"

"Restraining order. He's staying with his father."

Mike read the paper over and over. John's father was going to court.

"I'll leave now," Mike said. "You can fight this thing. With me gone he doesn't have a leg to stand on. I'll call."

It took three weeks for Janet to temporarily get John back. John's father was going to fight for full custody on the grounds that Janet was a lesbian, "evidenced by her apparent relationship with a lesbian referred to as Bear."

Mike stayed at hotels and friends' houses, always keeping her eyes open for subpoena servers. Her friend Leslie, a women's studies student, became her best source of support and only confidant.

"You have to leave town, Mike. I'm afraid they'll find you." Janet's voice was a mixture of fear and rage.

"How's John?"

"He's okay. He asked for you as soon as he came back. When he didn't see you here, he checked your room and asked me if you were gone. I said yes and he started crying. Then, all of a sudden, he just stopped. And you know what he said? He asked me if he could write you a letter in heaven. He said the only way you wouldn't be there is if you went to heaven ... over the rainbow."

Mike cried into the phone.

"Tell him I'm sorry, Janet. Please tell him I'm sorry."

"I think I'm just going to leave it as it is. He's dealing with it his own way. But you have to leave, Mike. If they subpoena you my lawyer says they'll win the case. He says one look at you will convince the jury."

"How does your lawyer know what I look like?"

"The teacher at John's school described you."

"Ask your lawyer for the description sometime. I'd love to hear how that broad described me. She didn't like me the moment she saw me."

"What about leaving, Mike? Will you go?"

"I'll spend a few weeks in New York City with a friend. I'll call and find out when it's safe to come back."

❏ ❏

Leslie invited Mike to her family's house in Flushing, and they spent the next two weeks falling in love. They were already friends; becoming lovers came almost naturally. They didn't talk about it, analyze it, or worry about it. They just melted into each other, accepting all the wonder and strength of their growing love.

Janet fought her case as a straight woman and spent much of her time talking negatively about gay people. Mike figured it was the best tactic, but others saw it differently.

"She'd have a better case if she fought it as a lesbian mother," Leslie said. "The defense fund would help her out."

"But I don't think she *is* a lesbian, honey." As Mike rubbed Leslie's back, she drank in all the feelings she'd missed for so long. "I don't think Janet can love anybody. She hates men. But hating men doesn't make her gay."

She turned Leslie over, savoring the feel of her skin. Leslie helped Mike out of her shirt, and quietly they touched and stroked, featherlike touches that lasted into the night.

"Don't ever stop touching me, Mike. I love your touches."

Mike knew deep in her heart that Leslie was the love she'd been waiting for.

THE PERSONAL
IS POLITICAL

Leslie was easy to love. She had a way about her that drew people, an honesty that made them trust her. She was also one of the most organized people Mike had ever met. Everything was on an agenda. Mike figured women's studies did that to you. Meetings and classes were always twice as long as they were supposed to be, and the whole program could fall apart if someone important lost her appointment book or phone list. Teaching women about themselves was complicated, and Mike enjoyed getting involved. In some ways, Mike felt at home, almost like she was back in the military. Though the women prided themselves on being Socialists and freethinkers, Mike saw them as very regimented and rigid. Once you were taught the rhetoric of the women's movement, you weren't allowed to stray or change the rules. There was no hierarchy, but those with the most theory were definitely in charge. Leslie was much more practiced than Mike was. She even held a meeting with Mike to discuss their relationship and living arrangements.

"I'd like us to live together," Mike said. "The only time we see each other is weekends and late at night. It makes sense to live together."

"But I'm a collective person," Leslie said. "I live collectively, with women's support."

"I can give you support. Or I can live collectively with you."

Leslie shook her head. "You don't understand. The women I live with are like me. Femmes, I guess. And we need space from our lovers sometimes. You need to find your own collective household."

Leslie set up a meeting between Mike and three women looking for a fourth to live in their house. Mike didn't care for the women very much, but if Leslie wanted her to try this collective living thing, she would. They all moved into a house on the opposite side of the city, but Mike spent every spare minute with Leslie. She waited at the college until the meetings were over and at Leslie's house while phone calls were made. She discussed the women's movement and Mao and Marx and struggled to learn what was politically correct. Mostly, she loved Leslie with every ounce of her being.

"I want to make love back to you," Leslie said. "I'm a woman who loves women, and you're a woman. I want to love you back."

"But no one's ever made love to me, and I don't want them to," Mike said. She felt threatened by this new side to their relationship. She always gave her lovers pleasure, and always she felt satisfied when her lovemaking satisfied them. No one had ever touched her. Her chest, her back, even her legs, but no one was allowed beyond that. And no one had ever seemed interested before. They loved her touches and attention. Leslie was the first to ask.

"I can't, honey. I've never been on the bottom. It just wouldn't feel right."

"We'll make it feel right. Being a feminist means loving yourself. And being a lesbian means loving women. I can't love you if you don't love the woman in you."

"Loving myself doesn't mean being on the bottom."

"But I want to give you pleasure, too."

"I get it. Loving you makes me happy. Making love to you gives me pleasure."

Mike kissed her slowly and deeply and, as always, that strangely wonderful sensation of absolute and total belonging overcame them so that they clung to each other breathlessly. It wasn't a needy kind of clinging. It was more an all-consuming power that made Mike know she could live without her, but she'd be damned if she was going to. They would often turn to each other in their sleep and embrace with that same power and passion, never waking or even opening their eyes, just holding and pouring into each other in their dreams. But now, Leslie was pushing for more.

"We'll get the massage book and light some candles. You'll be relaxed and it'll be wonderful. You'll see."

Leslie was her life. Mike couldn't deny her. The massage felt fine, until she felt Leslie's fingers gently tracing lines up and down her thighs. She wanted to roll on top of Leslie and love her as she always did, but Leslie kept one hand on her stomach to hold her down, silently telling her it was now or never.

Mike felt the aching fear of her vulnerability. It tensed her muscles, shook her, jerked her away from Leslie's touches. Her love was pulled from inside of her, no longer a secret mystery, an internal force, but now a physical power, external and almost unattached to her heart. She went to Leslie's kisses, came to her touch, and the strength that had sustained her for so long seemed to burst from her, crushing her and filling her until all she could do was cry in her lover's arms. The tears wouldn't stop. Being loved by a woman she loved thrust her into a world that wasn't hers. But it was Leslie's world, and God, how she loved her.

Buffalo's blizzard of 1977 caused death and destruction and a peculiar new disease called "cabin fever." Mike had started fasting the day before the blizzard hit to get rid of the few extra pounds that blissful love seemed to create. Leslie and her housemates cooked through five days of storms, and Mike felt lucky that the blizzard had come while she was with her lover. If she had been home, the endless days and nights

137

of snow and wind and the biting loneliness of not living with the one she loved would have been more devastating than the storm.

Together, they watched *Roots*, discussed racism, cuddled under blankets, and danced to Stevie Wonder and Diana Ross. They watched the cat have kittens, tried to define butch and femme, and made love until the snow stopped.

"Mike, we don't want you for a roommate anymore." Nancy sat erect and checked her notes to be sure she was covering the full agenda.

"You're never here, and we find you unsupportive. Though we've tried to give you constructive criticism and help you through the process of learning to live collectively, we don't see any change."

Mike maintained her relaxed yet controlled stance in the doorway and smiled at her roommate's coldness.

"Only a true feminist could be so cold and detached while sending another woman to the street," she said. "Sometimes I think you women masturbate too much or something." Then, to be sure she had the upper hand in a situation that would probably be too humiliating for some women to bear, she kissed the air and patted her butt as she left the room. She didn't like treating women that way, but the tone was much like her mother's and the reasoning much the same. Once again, she was being told to leave because she couldn't or wouldn't give enough of herself to a household. It hurt. But it was also an opportunity. Mike knew of a vacant apartment just a block from Leslie's house, and she longed to be closer. She needed to be closer. She almost feared not being closer. Leslie had too many people around her, too many followers, too many pseudo-mothers and -daughters. She was beautiful and radical and politically correct, and Mike was always afraid of losing her to someone who might be more feminine or womanly or whatever it was that lesbian-feminists wanted.

She took the lower corner apartment and relaxed in her solitude. Leslie wasn't happy about the way Mike had treated her old household, but she understood and forgave and even enjoyed being alone with Mike on alternate nights.

"I want to take you home to meet my parents," Mike said. "I don't know why, 'cause we haven't really spoken in years, but I want to show you off. I want them to know you're the one I'm going to spend my life with."

"I can handle that. We'll take pictures with us. The ones from camping at Letchworth, from the beach, from the trip to Maine. Pictures help break the ice. We'll stay a couple of hours, maybe have tea ... Oh, I'll bring the herb tea, then we'll..."

"Hold it! You can't have an agenda with my family!"

Mike almost laughed as she thought of Leslie trying to run a meeting with her mother.

"There's a lot of bad blood there. And it's their turf. As soon as my mother sees me, she'll have her own agenda."

Mike smiled as Leslie backed down from her women's studies mode. For once, Mike felt in control.

"My mother's really not that bad." She kept an arm around Leslie as they drove the thruway. When they neared Fredonia, she caught herself looking into cars. She wanted to see someone she knew. She wanted them to see her and Leslie together.

"I forgot to shave my legs," Leslie said.

"I don't mind. They won't notice."

"I don't like hair."

"Feminists don't shave, remember?"

"I don't shave a lot of the time because you never do."

"What do I have to do with it? It's your body. It's up to you."

"I'm trying to support you," Leslie said. "I don't want people thinking you're weird."

"I don't really care. I've never shaved and I never will. That's me, not you. If you wanna shave, shave."

"I did want to today, but I forgot."

Mike pulled the car to the side of the road, patted Leslie's leg, and hopped out. When she got back in, she handed Leslie a bouquet of wildflowers.

"I love you. Don't be nervous."

They drove by Betty's house, and Mike ducked so Betty wouldn't see her.

"I have to remember to write Betty a letter. She told me that when I knew who I was, and was committed to being me, I should let her know."

"Can I meet her?"

"I don't think so. It would hurt her too much. I'll tell her about you in a letter. We have a kind of agreement. If she writes back and wants to meet you, that's one thing. If she doesn't write back, well, that's another."

Mike watched the blood leave her father's face as he opened the door.

"Hi, Dad. This is Leslie. Mom home?"

"Jesus, Mary, and Joseph. You don't call. You don't write."

"We were in town and I thought it would be nice to stop in."

"Mr. Landetti, Mike's told me all about you. I feel like I know you already."

Leslie shook Al's hand and breezed in. Mike motioned to her father to follow, and the threesome made their way to the kitchen.

"I'm a little afraid of what Mike's told you. She can be a tough son of a..."

"Dad, relax. We're all older now. We just came to visit for a while."

"Don't worry, Mr. Landetti. Mike only says good things."

Al looked pleasantly surprised when Leslie patted him lovingly on the shoulder.

"Mike met my Dad. In New York. I'm crazy about my father. They got along fine."

"Except he thought I was a boy," Mike said.

"No, he didn't. What makes you think that?"

"You told him. He looked at you and said, 'Boy,' and you nodded your head yes."

Leslie thought for a moment and laughed.

"He didn't call you a boy. He was asking if you were a goy. Goy! That means not Jewish!"

140

Mike felt her face reddening. She wanted to laugh but was afraid she was on the thin edge between laughing and crying. Her father broke the ice with his own outburst. He was a great laugher when he let himself go, and this was as good a time as any.

"Ha, ha. Poor Mike. You thought he called you a boy?"

Mike felt the tears well in her eyes and tried to laugh them away with her father. Before long, they were both near hysteria, alternately wiping away tears and doubling up with laughter. In a flash, their natural bond sucked them into an embrace and the laughter turned to sobs.

"We always loved you, Michaelene. We always loved you."

Mike felt her love for him, but couldn't tell him. There was too much pain blocking the words. They hugged and cried and then backed away cautiously, as if both were afraid of revealing too much.

"You must be Mike's mom. I'm Leslie."

They shook hands, and Mike watched in amazement as Leslie immediately took over the kitchen and got everyone settled for coffee and tea. They sat opposite Mike's parents and gently touched their feet together under the table. The tension was so great that each time Leslie touched Mike's foot, Mike had an overwhelming urge to grab her and make love to her right there, in the kitchen, in front of everyone. She laughed to herself as she calmed her stomach with warm sips of coffee. Passion was such a strange emotion. It had a life of its own, sometimes totally separate from love, entangled and caught up with fear and hate and anger. She was amazed Leslie's touches still aroused her they way they did after almost three years of constant love. She had always thought passion disappeared much quicker than that.

Happily, she waved good-bye to her parents and raced up Maple Avenue faster than the law allowed. She screeched to a stop at the corner and pulled Leslie to her. They cried into each other's arms as the terrible rigidity of family and anger and fear eased from their bodies.

"I love you, honey. With all my heart. I love you."

"I love you, too, Mike."

Leslie stayed next to her as they made the hour-long trip back to Buffalo. Both had wanted to stay and make love in the car, but they also wanted to get away from the pressures of Fredonia. They caressed and kissed at sixty miles per hour until Leslie said she couldn't stand it anymore. She undid her jeans and leaned back in the seat so Mike could love her at high speed. Each time Leslie gasped, Mike had to remind herself to ease up on the accelerator. Her own passion and her utter connection to Leslie's pleasure made her body move with her lover's and her power surge through her legs. By the time they reached the toll booth, they both felt the cooling wetness that eases the fever of a love too strong. They settled in with Diana Ross for the final mile home and the "Sweetest Hangover."

❏ ❏

The letter to Betty was hard to write. Mike knew Betty would be hurt, but they had an agreement and Mike cared enough to honor it. She didn't want to lose Betty. She still loved her dearly, and even Leslie hadn't taken her place in her heart. But she had to be truthful. She had often gone home to Betty's when Leslie was too busy coordinating women's studies or taking "femme space." Each time, she pretended that nothing had changed and Betty was still number one. Each time, she felt guilty. She wrote gently and directly, with every bit of reassurance she could muster. The bang of the mailbox made her decision final.

❏ ❏

"So, who can take me to lunch?"

Ana's shortness and Chilean accent made her request almost childlike, and Mike couldn't resist.

"I'll see how long Leslie's gonna be," Mike said.

"Oh, well, then I'll get my coat. This is women's studies. The clock is like a man. It has no voice."

Mike peeked into the meeting and Leslie waved her away. That usually meant it would be hours before anyone escaped from the room, and everyone in the meeting was doing their usual constant snacking anyway.

"Come on, little woman. It's you and me."

"I am not so little."

Mike chuckled as she politely held the door for Ana.

"And look at you," Ana said. "You walk tall, but you're not so much taller."

They drove to a nearby deli and had a strangely silent lunch. Ana seemed full of energy but stayed nervously quiet while they ate.

"Can you take me home?" Ana asked. "I live in the building you are in."

"You do?" Mike was surprised. "I've never seen you there."

"That's because you don't use your third eye. Your mind is too busy. I've seen you. Amalia has seen you."

"Amalia?"

"My daughter."

"A little kid? About so big? With big, beautiful brown eyes and dimples?"

"Why does everyone seem so little to you? Yes. Amalia. The one you pay special attention to each morning as you leave. But she is only seven, so forget it."

"Forget what?"

"Never mind. I know. After all, I'm Chilean. *Quiere café?*"

"Sure."

"Aha! I knew it. I just knew it."

"Knew what?" Mike could only laugh. This was one of the most apolitical and crazy conversations she'd had in a long time.

"You understood. I knew you would. You have Latin blood. That's why the ladies love you."

"What ladies?"

"Uh-uh. Don't kid me. You know."

"Know what? Geez. What the hell? I don't even know you."

"You know me. And you know how to talk to the ladies. And you know Spanish. Come. I'll give you your coffee and Amalia can see your eyes."

143

Ana and Amalia greeted each other in Spanish and English, and Mike immediately fell in love with Amalia's dimpled smile.

"I like the little cups," Mike said as Ana poured.

"Again with the 'little' business. This is how we drink our coffee in Chile. Someday you'll go there and you'll see."

They drank their coffee with a mystifying warmth and an intriguing silence. It wasn't that Mike didn't know what to say, it was more that she felt she didn't have to say it. There was a quiet understanding between them, and Mike wasn't surprised when they finished at exactly the same time and pushed their cups together to the middle of the table.

"You have to go now," Ana said. "I have company coming."

She led Mike to the door and leaned against it almost seductively.

"Now you know where we live. Use your third eye and learn."

As always, Mike made sure she wasn't too busy to greet Leslie at the door when she finally came home.

"Guess who lives upstairs? On the third floor? That Ana woman from the college. With her little kid."

"Is that why you weren't there to pick me up and you didn't answer your phone?"

"I thought you waved me away. I went to lunch with her."

"I think I need some space tonight," Leslie said. "And I've been thinking about all the time we spend together. I'd like to have a couple of nights a week and maybe one weekend a month to be with my friends."

Mike felt like Leslie had just punched her in the mouth. "What's the matter? You're mad that I had lunch with someone? You have lunch with people every day."

"I'm not mad. In fact, I think it's good for you. We spend too much time together, that's all. I need to be with my friends. It doesn't mean I don't love you."

"Well it sure as hell means something. I don't think we spend too much time together. Sometimes I feel like I never see you. What the hell am I supposed to do while you're taking all this space?"

144

"Take some space for yourself."

"I don't need any space. Space is for space cadets. Four years, and suddenly you need more space."

"Don't make a big deal out of it. I have more work at the college now, and it's hard to maintain so many relationships. We'll love each other better this way."

"I thought we were loving each other fine, except we had too much space from each other and too many people around all the time. I thought it would be better if we lived together so we wouldn't have to juggle our schedules so much."

"Look, I'm just asking for a little space. We're going to the music festival pretty soon and A Woman's Place; that'll be quality time."

Mike tried to pull Leslie close for a long good-bye kiss, but Leslie wouldn't give in. Leslie was probably right, Mike decided, feeling she didn't have any other choice. She made her bed on the couch and watched television until she fell asleep.

In the morning, she made up her mind to start putting her career first. She had finished college, but the degree wasn't the magic paper it was supposed to have been. Her job at the computing center paid well and gave her good benefits. She'd sink her teeth into her work, be there when Leslie needed her, and try to build some security for herself.

She and Dick managed the lab, a place where sick terminals and minicomputers came for repair. They designed and installed a telecommunications system for the university and sometimes worked day and night to keep it up and running.

Dick was a tall ex-Navy man with a moustache and an insatiable desire to get ahead. Though Mike had seven years more experience, they both started at essentially the same salary. It wasn't long before Dick was made the director and Mike only the manager.

"After all," Dick explained, "people will listen to me and trust what I say. You're a team player. If we're going to build this into a functional part of the university, we have to have leadership. Your pay won't be far behind mine. Before long, we'll be hiring more guys to take over the dirty work, and you'll be in charge."

Mike wore her beeper everywhere, which made it very convenient when Leslie, Amalia, or Ana wanted to reach her, or someone from women's studies needed a ride or a favor. At times, it seemed to be the busiest beeper in Buffalo.

"Okay, kid. I got your beep and came home for lunch. What's up?"

Amalia carefully unwrapped a messy peanut butter sandwich and placed it in front of Mike. She was seven and on her own in the afternoon while Ana taught at the college. Mike smiled at her grown-up attitude, but was careful not to mock her or laugh at her.

"I wanted to have a talk with you," Amalia said. "About some stuff at school."

"Okay. Whenever you're ready."

Mike didn't like peanut butter, at least not without jelly, but she bit into the sandwich and tried to hide the fact that it immediately stuck to the roof of her mouth.

"What's capitalism?"

Mike nodded and tried to get the gooeyness away from her teeth so she could talk.

"Capitalism? Well, a system that helps the rich get richer by putting the workers in positions that don't pay them for their work while they produce a lot of meaningless things that break and we're all convinced we need so that we buy them with whatever money we have left after taxes. How's that? Does that make sense?"

Amalia nodded. Mike was glad that she didn't have to repeat her explanation. She wasn't sure what she had said.

"And what's a worker?"

"A worker is someone chained to her job by need, who never gets paid what she's worth, pays the government for benefits she'll never get to use, and buys back everything other workers make so that the rich get richer."

"Oh." Amalia diligently chewed her own sandwich and Mike marveled at how children's mouths seemed to be wetter or something so that peanut butter didn't stick as much.

146

"So what's this all about, Squirt? You're not worried about capitalism, are ya?"

"Uh-huh. I don't wanna be a worker. But I don't wanna be one of the rich guys with chains, either."

"Seems like a lot to worry about when you're only seven."

"My mother says it's because I'm Chilean. We need to worry about stuff like this."

"Well, your mother's your mother, but I've got a secret for you. It won't do any good to worry about it. Your mother teaches in a place where grown-ups worry about it and talk about it all the time, but you know what? They buy newspapers and books and records that teach them about capitalism, and they spend a lot of money. Then they eat all day while they discuss it and worry about it until they get so upset that they have to make themselves feel better. Then what do you think they do? They go shopping. They buy clothes and jewelry and albums and cars and stereos and televisions and cameras and more food, and then they feel better."

"So the workers weren't unpaloyed and the rich got richer?"

"Right. Except it's unemployed and that's what I'll be if I don't get back to work. Come on down later and we'll buy some cheap popcorn and watch television together."

"That's why my mother won't buy a television. She doesn't want that General to get richer."

"What General?"

"Lectric. She says General Lectric will get richer, so she won't buy one."

"So that's why you're down at my house all the time."

"No. My mother says you have Chilean blood and she trusts you. So I trust you, too."

"And you like television."

"Right."

Mike knelt to her level and got her daily big squeeze. Amalia was a special kid with a courage Mike adored. Sometimes, it hurt to be with her because it reminded her

147

of John, but mostly, they just had fun together. Often, Ana joined them when Leslie wasn't around.

It seemed Leslie's life was busier than ever. Mike tried to participate in the college as much as she could by joining the rallies and marches, speaking in classes, and working on committees, but her time with Leslie was limited, and Leslie was close to graduating. Change was in the air every time they spoke. Leslie was unsure of her future, afraid of what would happen to her when she was no longer a student and involved with women's studies. She had to find a career that made sense to her after years of politics and working with women.

Mike understood her panic, but she tried to reassure her.

"You don't have to rush into anything," she said. "I'll take care of money stuff, and when the right thing comes along, you'll be ready for it."

Still, Leslie needed space. When they were together, Mike took extra time to savor loving her. She bought a king-size waterbed that would keep them warm in the winter and would ease the tensions that wouldn't go away. She stayed up all night Christmas Eve waiting for it to fill up, only to realize that such a large bed would take days to get warm.

She took Leslie dancing and to concerts and camping in the forest so they could make love among the pine trees. She bought her earrings shaped like women's symbols, politically correct t-shirts, a suit she could use for interviews, and flowers on every rainy day. She bared her chest at A Woman's Place and massaged Leslie in the sun. She flew her to St. Augustine to lie naked on the beach. And almost every night, she went home alone so that Leslie could have her space, be with her friends, and go through whatever process she needed to make her stronger.

"I'm applying to chiropractic school," Leslie said.

"Great. That's a great idea. Chiropractors aren't screwed up, and some of them believe in vitamins and health food. That's a great idea."

"But all the schools are west of here. And it takes two years. You'll have to quit your job."

"Oh. I don't know, honey. I don't know if I can do that."

"I'll need you with me. And I'll need help paying for school."

"Then what? When school is done, what happens then?"

"Then I find a place to practice."

"So I quit another job and move again?"

"You're employable. Computers are everywhere."

Mike thought about all the work she had done at the center. Her job seemed easy now. It didn't seem right to quit and start over, but she didn't want Leslie to go without her, either. She felt like a housewife following her husband wherever his job took him.

"I don't know, Les. I have to think about it."

"You have to think kinda quick. My application's due in three weeks."

The first week sped by as Mike struggled to understand Leslie's needs. Mike wasn't as employable as Leslie thought. She was highly skilled and educated, but she was also a dyke, and looked like one. It wasn't easy interviewing and getting hired. She didn't know who to talk to. All her friends were Leslie's friends, and she couldn't put them in the middle. She wanted to call Betty, but she had never answered Mike's letter and Mike had to respect her decision. She went to Ana.

"Why do you fight with a decision like this?" she said. "You Americans are crazy. Crazy! In Chile, we would never ask this of someone."

"I don't think it's an American problem. I think it's just men and femmes."

"It shouldn't be a problem. If Leslie wants to do this, then she has to find the way. If she loves you, she'll stay true to you and come to you when she can. You make people dependent on you, Chiquitita. They shouldn't be dependent. It only makes you feel guilty when you can't do what they want."

"But if we were straight and married..."

"Then you would be the husband and she would follow you."

"But that's not feminist."

"And neither is her demand of you."

Mike went to Ana's every night and talked until early morning. Ana told her about Chilean oppression and the difference between theory and living. She shared secrets about Allende and the coup and the junta, and drew her pictures of the country.

"You need to follow your heart, Mike, but also your history. You weren't meant to live everyone else's lives. Your third eye will tell you."

They hugged a friendly hug, and Ana looked deeply into Mike's eyes. "Your blood is hot, like mine. You feel things without reading. The land is a part of you, the stars listen to you, and the moon breathes with you. Even Amalia knows this about you. If you need Leslie, you will go with her. If you love her, you will let her go without you."

Mike was lost in Ana's words as she drove to Leslie's house for their prearranged meeting. Leslie's agenda was clear: Mike had to have either an answer or a way to find one. Mike had neither.

"I think we have to go to counseling, Mike. Couples counseling. So we can figure out what to do."

"I don't believe in that stuff. People talk themselves into things."

"It's the only way I know. Unless there's someone else, and that's the reason you're undecided."

"There's no one else, honey. It's just hard to keep starting over."

Three nights later, they had their first counseling session. Mike told Leslie to start, because she had no idea what she was supposed to talk about. Leslie spoke about her dreams and her political decision to pursue a chiropractic career. When it was Mike's turn, she could only say she was confused. She wanted to be with her lover, but she didn't want to quit her job. When they were finished, the counselor summarized Leslie's feelings first.

"You, my dear, are just fine. You have direction and purpose and your stuff is together. You don't need me."

She smiled at Leslie, who seemed pleased with her analysis, and then turned to Mike. "But you, I need to see some more. You have some baggage, some deep-rooted problem we have to get to. It'll take us a while to push it out."

"What should we do in the meantime?" Leslie asked.

"I think you both need space from this problem."

Mike looked at the ceiling. She still couldn't understand why everyone always needed this thing called space. Why couldn't they just deal with things head-on?

"You should both stay away from each other for a while, and Mike should see me a few times over the next couple of weeks. Leslie should go do what she has to do and keep on pluggin' at those goals."

Mike wanted to spend time with Leslie after the session, but Leslie was convinced they should do as the counselor said, and stay away from each other. Mike had to hold back her tears.

"Why do we suddenly have problems? This isn't a relationship problem. It's a business decision. I don't think we should do this separately, honey. I need you."

"Don't worry," Leslie said as she closed the door. "It'll all work out."

Mike started for her apartment door, but went instead up to Ana's. Nothing made sense to her. Leslie was personalizing something that was more a problem of logistics and gay oppression. It made Mike angry that a stranger's comments were just accepted and acted on, as if being a social worker gave you a license to destroy lives.

Ana met her in the hallway and took her hands.

"I knew you were coming. I have company, so we'll talk here."

Mike couldn't say anything. She felt her love for Leslie choking her as it shattered into tiny pieces and inched its way up her throat.

"Oh, no, Chiquitita. You fill your eyes with oceans of pain and cloud your mind's eye so that it cannot see. Move away from this pain. Fill your heart with gladness and laughter, so you can see the answer better."

Mike swallowed hard and hugged her friend. She wanted to cry, to be held, to have someone with her so it didn't hurt so much.

"Mike?"

She jumped at the sound of Leslie's voice.

"I came to tell you I'm going to New York for a week. To think about things."

Guiltily, Mike pulled away from Ana. She could only nod her head in understanding.

"We'll talk when I get back," Leslie said. She smiled at Ana before heading back down the stairs.

"She doesn't know what she's losing," Ana said. "Come for dinner tomorrow. We'll have Chilean stew."

Mike spent the week working and visiting with Ana. She didn't like going home to her empty bed, and she couldn't sleep. She was exhausted, but she felt less angry. She greeted Leslie at the door cautiously and kept her distance, though all she really wanted to do was hold her and pull her back to make things the way they were.

"I had an affair in New York, Mike. I thought you should hear it from me before it gets through the grapevine."

Mike felt her heart die in the pit of her stomach, but she stayed calm and strong to try to show Leslie it was okay. She wanted her to know it wouldn't change things, that she'd still love her as much as ever. But her brain and her mouth didn't agree.

"I did, too," she said.

Leslie looked at her knowingly, almost victoriously.

"I knew that, Mike. With Ana. That's why I did it."

Mike felt trapped. She hadn't really done anything with anyone. She wanted Leslie to hurt the same way she did, and she couldn't make herself back down.

"That's great. I hope it made you feel good."

Mike was triumphant. She saw the pain in Leslie's eyes, and she knew she had finally struck a blow. Part of her wanted to stop the game, quickly, before the hurt had a chance to settle in, but another part of her, somewhere closer to her soul, closer to the heart that had loved this woman so deeply, wanted to inflict the pain, to turn the knife slowly, as it had turned in her. Leslie was hurt. As Leslie turned to leave, Mike felt herself gasping to call after her, but the door closed and it was too late.

MUSIC
LADY

Mike took the week off from work and cried herself dry. Ana and Amalia tried to visit, but she told them she needed space. She laughed as she realized she finally understood what that meant. The night before Leslie's application had to be done, Mike made her decision. Leslie was out somewhere and the thought of her not hearing Mike's answer immediately scared Mike into writing a letter.

> Honey,
> I was a fool to ever put a job on the same plane as my love for you. You're more important than any job, and starting over means nothing when you do it with someone you truly love. I'm sorry for all the mess I've caused, for all the tears. I'll go with you, wherever you have to go. Please read this and come back to me. I'll be waiting for you. I love you for all that you are and all you'll ever be.

She taped the letter to Leslie's door and went home to wait for her lover's call. She was glad it was over. Even though moving would be hard and their lifestyle would drastically change, she was glad they'd do it together. She wondered if Leslie would still want as much space. She worried that they would again have to live apart, that Leslie would want another collective household. But it didn't matter. Leslie was her lover, and nothing else mattered.

Mike answered the phone so quickly, it barely had a chance to ring. She lowered her voice, calmed it, so Leslie would know and feel that everything was okay.

"Mike? I got your letter."

"I would have told you in person, but I didn't know what time you'd be home. I wanted you to know as soon as you got in."

"I'm sorry I wasn't here."

"That's okay. I know you're busy."

"Well, the reason I wasn't here is that I've been seeing someone new."

Mike put a shaking hand on her heart and silently shook her head. She didn't want to hear what was coming next.

"Mike? I don't want to hurt this woman. Maybe if you had decided sooner, I don't know. But I think I'm in love with her. I couldn't hurt her now."

Mike grabbed the receiver with both hands. She wanted to slam it, throw it, crush the voice on the other end.

"You've only known her a couple of weeks," Mike said. "Didn't you tell her you were in a relationship and we were trying to work things out?"

"I don't know what I told her. I just know I can't hurt her."

"Let me come over. I wanna see you."

"No! Maybe tomorrow. Maybe we can figure out how to still be friends."

"What about your precious school? When do you have to leave?"

"I decided not to go. I'm going to stay here and figure out what to do. I'll call you tomorrow."

The dial tone stayed in Mike's ear for what seemed like a lifetime. She ripped the phone from the wall and hurled it against the stereo. Twice and again, she started for her car to go to Leslie's, but each time she turned around. If she

155

went now, they'd fight for sure. She'd have no chance of showing Leslie how wrong she was. She'd wait, and kill her with kindness. The affair would pass, and Leslie would come to her senses.

In the days that followed, Mike tried everything to get her lover back. She massaged her, listened, gently asked questions about the other woman. They still had tickets to Diana Ross, and Leslie said because it was Valentine's Day, they should go to the concert. All through the evening, they held hands and swayed and sang to each other. Leslie's friends were behind and in front, checking constantly, sometimes smiling at the two they always called the "beautiful couple," but also frowning, as if warning Leslie that she shouldn't get too close. When Diana sang "Sweetest Hangover," Mike and Leslie cried into each other's shoulder. They still loved each other, neither could deny it.

When they drove back from their three hours of loving, they still stayed close in the car. The radio played "Reunited," and Mike held Leslie's hand with all the love that flowed from her.

"Can you drop me at the bar?"

Mike didn't really want to be in a gay bar right then, but if that's what Leslie wanted, she'd go.

"I didn't think we were going out after the concert," Mike said.

"I'm meeting someone there."

Mike pulled over to the curb.

"You mean the new one? Micki? You're meeting her now?"

"She let me go to the concert with you, Mike. I told her I'd meet her."

"*Let* you go? You mean you asked her permission and she *let* you go? Jesus Christ, honey, what the hell are you doin'?"

"You shouldn't call me that anymore, Mike. I told you I wouldn't hurt this woman."

"After everything we just felt? After everything we've been through together? You just want to throw it all away on some goddam woman who *lets* you go out with your lover."

"I'll get out here."

"I hope she bites your neck off!" Mike shouted as Leslie slammed the door. Leslie self-consciously covered the passion mark that Mike had had to look at all evening and then disappeared from Mike's life.

Mike's anger was too great for tears. She drove like a crazy woman, speeding up and down streets, squealing her tires around corners. She went through a red light, almost broadsiding another car.

"I don't want to die," she said to herself. "No one is worth killing yourself over. Slow down, dummy, before you hurt someone else."

She drove slowly to Leslie's house and sat outside to calm herself. "Cathy's Clown" played on the radio, and then "Dream, Dream, Dream." Mike could only shake her head and laugh.

"Just what I needed. An Everly Brothers double to make my night."

She went home to her couch and thought about break-ups, how much like death they seemed. She looked through old photo albums and read old letters, but she couldn't cry. Crying would make it too final, and she never wanted that. A picture of John with his Christmas train tugged at a part of her she had hidden away. A Popsicle wrapper near a picture of Sharon made her think of first love and if any love ever lasted. Betty's gleaming smile made her go to the phone to call. Betty might not want to talk to her, but she'd be polite, and Mike only wanted to hear her voice.

"Hello, Betty?"

"Uh, no, no. Who's this?"

"Mike. Is Betty there?"

"Just a minute."

The strange voice whispered to someone close to her, and Mike strained to hear what they were saying.

"Mike? It's Bob. How the hell are ya, kid?"

"I'm okay. Betty doesn't want to talk to me, right?"

"Betty's dead, Mike. She died three weeks ago. Aneurysm."

"Oh, God, no! Why didn't someone tell me? I would have been there. Why didn't someone tell me?"

"We thought you knew, Mike. We figured you didn't come because you couldn't. You know, as close as you were."

"I have to hang up, Bob. I'm sorry."

"She didn't forget ya, Mike. I wasn't there because, you know, I had someone else. But everyone remembers how it happened. She bought a beer at the Inn and had just toasted you. She said, 'Here's to the kid,' and then fell off the bar stool. She died right away, Mike. She didn't suffer."

The tears came freely when Mike hung up. Betty's death was final, a relationship she could never hope for anymore. She banged her head on the wall and screamed at God. She begged Betty to forgive her for not being there for her. She sunk to her knees as she held the wall, the only true support she felt, and cried through the night until, mercifully, she slept.

She woke before the sun did and robotically went upstairs to Ana. She didn't know what time it was, and she didn't care. She needed family, someone to care for her, and Ana was all she had.

It was still dark when Ana answered the door, but she didn't ask questions or act surprised. She hardly even blinked. She simply led Mike to bed, then held her into the morning.

❏ ❏

"My poor little bootch," Ana said as she stroked Mike's head to wake her.

"Butch. It's butch, not bootch." Mike smiled into the eyes of the loving woman next to her as Amalia came in and joined them in bed.

"Hi, Mike. I knew it was you under the covers. What's a bootch?"

Amalia lay down on Mike's other side, and Mike put an arm around both of them and held them close.

"A butch is someone no one understands and no one can explain," she said. She thought about answering better, but

158

she wasn't sure anyone could really truthfully say. "Some people think she's mannish, but she really isn't, and being like a man is the furthest thing from her mind. Some people think it's a role that you play, like acting, pretending to be what a man might be in a relationship with a woman. But it's not acting, or playing, or a role. It's being a kid and old at the same time. It's loving women with a part of you no man will ever discover and other women will never find. It's not even really being a dyke or queer or a lesbian. Femmes are those things. It's being a feminist without needing a definition or an analysis. It's loving women without needing to be told how. It's having control when you really don't and being tough when you really aren't and giving love when you really can't and surviving in a world that doesn't want you to and dressing so men don't mistake you for prey and walking in a way that keeps you alive."

"Whatever you say, Mike," Amalia smirked.

"I have a tape downstairs by a woman named Madeline Davis. If you listen to the refrain of the song, you'll understand better than most what a butch is."

"You get the tape and I'll make breakfast," Amalia said as she hopped off the bed.

"As long as it's not peanut butter, Squirt."

❏ ❏

> *Oh, she walks in boots of leather,*
> *and slippers made of gold.*
> *She'll be a child forever,*
> *and forever she'll be old.*
> *She's the heroine of legends,*
> *she's the eagle and the dove.*
> *She's the daughter of the moon.*
> *She's my sister and my love.*

The tape continued playing as Mike ate soggy eggs and settled into being with her new temporary family. She liked Madeline's voice and she liked the way many people treated her like a star. She thought of the first time they'd met. Mike

159

had kissed her hand and stared like a high school kid on a first date. Madeline was nothing like Sharon. In fact, she was probably like no one else Mike knew. She could never have Sharon again, but...

"Earth to Mike. Earth to Mike."

Amalia's smile and Ana's eyes broke Mike's daydream. She was better now. She'd heal. She'd go on. And someday, she'd fall in love again.